This Was Something Else Again, Something Beyond Her Experience, Something Pure, Wild, Right, Wrong.

She had no idea how long the kiss lasted. Time gave way to sensation and had no meaning. It was Devon who pulled back, pushed away. He was breathing heavily, his eyes so bright they blazed like beacons in the night.

"I think that answers your questions about us, don't you?" Devon asked. Then he headed for the door.

Brooke followed him. "Where are you going?" she asked. "You can't ride that Jet Ski in the dark—it's too dangerous out there."

He slid the door open and stepped outside, picking up his wet suit on the way. "Not as dangerous as in here, babe. Not by half."

Dear Reader,

Welcome to the merry month of May, where things here at Silhouette Desire get pretty perky. Needless to say, I think May's lineup of sexy heroes and spunky heroines is just fabulous...beginning with our star hunk, *Man of the Month* Cooper Maitland, in Jennifer Greene's *Quicksand*. This is one man you won't want to let get away!

Next, we have the second in Joan Johnston's HAWK'S WAY series, *The Cowboy and the Princess*. Now, please don't worry if you didn't read Book One, all of the HAWK'S WAY stories stand alone as great romantic reads.

Then the ever-popular Mary Lynn Baxter returns with *Mike's Baby* and Cait London appears with *Maybe No, Maybe Yes*. Maybe *you* won't want to miss *either* of these books! And don't pass up *Devil or Angel* by Audra Adams—just which best describes the hero, well, *I'm* not telling. Next, Carla Cassidy makes her Silhouette Desire debut with *A Fleeting Moment*. You'll never forget this witty, wonderful love story.

Yes, May is merry and filled with mayhem, but more important, it's filled with romance...only from Silhouette Desire. So, enjoy!

All the best,

Lucia Macro
Senior Editor

AUDRA ADAMS
DEVIL OR ANGEL

SILHOUETTE *Desire*®
Published by Silhouette Books New York
America's Publisher of Contemporary Romance

SILHOUETTE BOOKS
300 East 42nd St., New York, N.Y. 10017

DEVIL OR ANGEL

Copyright © 1993 by Marie D. Tracy

All rights reserved. Except for use in any review, the reproduction or utilization of this work in whole or in part in any form by any electronic, mechanical or other means, now known or hereafter invented, including xerography, photocopying and recording, or in any information storage or retrieval system, is forbidden without the permission of the publisher, Silhouette Books, 300 E. 42nd St., New York, N.Y. 10017

ISBN: 0-373-05783-0

First Silhouette Books printing May 1993

All the characters in this book have no existence outside the imagination of the author and have no relation whatsoever to anyone bearing the same name or names. They are not even distantly inspired by any individual known or unknown to the author, and all incidents are pure invention.

® and ™:Trademarks used with authorization. Trademarks indicated with ® are registered in the United States Patent and Trademark Office, the Canada Trade Mark Office and in other countries.

Printed in the U.S.A.

Books by Audra Adams

Silhouette Desire

Blue Chip Bride #532
People Will Talk #592
Home Sweet Home #695
Devil or Angel #783

AUDRA ADAMS

loves to dream up her characters' stories while lying on the beach on hot summer days. Luckily, her Jersey shore home offers her the opportunity to indulge in her fantasies.

She believes that falling in love is one of the most memorable experiences in a person's life. Young or old, male or female, we all can relate to those exquisitely warm feelings. She knows that stories of romance enable us to tap into that hidden pleasure and relive it through the characters.

An incurable romantic, Audra is in love with love, and hopes to share that optimism with each and every one of her readers.

To my "devil and angel," my children—
the real Adam and Audra

One

The late summer sky over Lenape Bay was smeared with shades of purple, pink and blue. Brooke Wallace lifted her face to catch the fading rays of the sun as she sped down Dune Road in her red sports convertible.

It had been a long trip, and she was tired. A week had passed since she'd left home for the state's mayors' convention, and it seemed an eternity. The work had been exhausting, the meetings endless.

She despised being cooped up in conference rooms, but that was especially true this time of year. Labor Day represented the official end of the summer season in the resort community of Lenape Bay, the day when all the "pigeons" left, and the townspeople returned to the less chaotic business of living.

Brooke loved early autumn on the bay. It was the time when the beach was all but deserted and her attic apartment free of the summer renters she grudgingly permitted to supplement her income. It was that very special season-with-no-name that fell in between the waning days of summer and the late October north winds.

Resenting the time away was about all she could do. Participation in the convention had been important, even vital, if Lenape Bay, or any of the bay towns for that matter, was to survive another year.

Brooke sighed. The problems seemed insurmountable. Each of the five towns in her area were experiencing the same depressing effects of the slow economy. Even though the figures for this last season were slightly better than the one before, there remained only a guarded optimism that there might be a light at the end of the tunnel. People still remembered the pollution problem on the shoreline a few years ago. They had taken a beating in the press, and the public had stayed away in droves. Brooke knew it would take only the smallest rumor of any perceived imperfection to see a return of the vultures swarming over the area, licking their lips in anticipation of an imminent feast.

She couldn't let that happen. Lenape Bay was her home. She was born, raised and, if you discounted those few years away at college and her brief stab at the holy state of matrimony, had spent all of her thirty-three years here. After her divorce five years ago, she'd returned to Lenape Bay. Her ex-husband, Andrew, had never liked small-town life, and she'd hated living in Boston. It had always been a bone of contention between them, one of many, she realized now. Coming home had afforded her the opportunity to redefine herself in a comfortable and secure setting.

A teacher by profession, her first two years were spent as vice-principal of the Lenape Bay elementary school. It had been a transitional time in her life when old dreams were put to rest and new ones needed to take their place.

Lenape Bay had been forced into change, as well, with the sudden death of Mayor Horace Leach, who had been a fixture in the town for forty years. At that time some members of the council had approached Brooke to run for the vacant office. They'd said they wanted her to be more active and involved than old Horace had ever been. They'd also wanted new blood and new ideas to revitalize the town.

While the thought had appealed to Brooke, she had been initially reluctant to make such a commitment. That was until her father had put in his two cents. With his usual bluster, Chaz Pattersen had persuaded her to run. "Meet the challenge," he'd said, and she had. No one on her election team had worked harder or been more supportive than he... and no one had been as proud as he when she'd taken the oath of office.

Three years ago Chaz had a fatal heart attack soon after her election. Brooke tucked a strand of windswept hair from her eyes as she remembered him. Without a doubt, her father had always been *the* force to be reckoned with in Lenape Bay. He had been a formidable personality in every sense of the word, having formed Pattersen Central Bank when he was only thirty years old. No one denied that he'd taken Lenape Bay from a sleepy bay town to a thriving resort community during his heyday.

Brooke could still remember walking down Main Street with him when she was a little girl. People would practically bow and scrape as they passed. Chaz had had an aura around him, one that demanded respect and accepted nothing less than excellence and blind obedience.

No one knew that better than Brooke and her brother Chuck. Chaz ran his family the same way he ran the bank: with total involvement. Brooke's only memory of her late mother had been from her pictures that had adorned the walls of the big house on the bay. Chaz had more than made up for any lack of maternal attention Brooke might have felt. She'd loved him dearly, and missed him still, though as an adult she could now admit that at times his obsession with control had been smothering.

There were moments, especially lately, when she wished he were still around. Chaz would have known how to fix things in town. He'd have known how to take charge and turn the tide of gloom that had settled over everyone. She loved her brother, but had admitted to herself a long time ago that Chuck had not inherited Chaz's business acumen. Since her father's death, Chuck had managed to undo most of what Chaz had taken a lifetime to build.

In all fairness, Brooke couldn't place the entire blame on Chuck. Chaz obviously hadn't intended to die when he did. He'd left a tangled mess of bank and personal business that the two of them were only now starting to unravel. She sighed. It seemed that the town of Lenape Bay and the Pattersen family were both in need of a miracle.

The sun was sinking fast, as it always did this time of year. Brooke pressed down on the accelerator in an attempt to beat the sunset to her door. As was her habit whenever she passed her old home, Brooke glanced toward the huge Victorian that sat on stilts on the bay. Chuck called it a "pink elephant," too big to maintain and impossible to rent. With all their financial problems, the house was expendable, and they had put it up for sale soon after Chaz's death.

But she had always loved the place, and she cherished the years she'd spent growing up there. Though she'd never discussed it with Chuck, she harbored a secret hope that no one would buy it, that she'd be able to come up with the money to refurbish it and live in it once again.

Brooke was just about to turn her attention back to the road when she did a double take and slammed her foot onto the brake. The car skidded to a halt on the dirt road, coughing up a spew of dust that made her sneeze.

Wiping her eyes, she stared at the light in the front parlor window. No movement was visible, but a green Jaguar was parked at the end of the driveway. She released the brake and put the car in reverse to get a closer look. The place was still. Slipping the car back into gear, she coasted to the end of the crushed-rock driveway. With one graceful motion, she was out of the car and up on the front porch peering inside. The heavy wooden door was wide open with only a dirty, dented screen door blocking her way.

"Hello?" she called. No one answered.

She wondered who could be at the house at this hour. The Realtor perhaps? There had been only a flicker of interest in the house and that had been during the first months the listing had hit the market. Now it sat tall and alone on the bay, weather-beaten and in need of much more work than either she or Chuck could afford. It had become what many felt was an eyesore—a big, lumbering, four-story, faded pink-and-gray Victorian on stilts.

Brooke looked over her shoulder, and her heart sank. The For Sale sign was gone. Who could have come out of the woodwork at this late date to buy it?

She knocked. No sounds answered her, no shuffling feet or movements of any kind came from within. Brooke opened the screen door. She fought an uneasy feeling as she stepped inside. She had a right to be here if only to help the sale along, she told her sinking stomach.

The house was empty. She strolled through each of the downstairs rooms calling out, but to no response. She couldn't help but touch a cloth-covered couch or table as she passed by. She and Chuck had decided to sell it lock, stock and barrel, not having the heart to throw out the old furniture, yet not having any use for it themselves.

Her ears pricked up at a far-off whirring noise like that of a motorboat. She followed the sound to the kitchen. The back door was open, with only the frame of an old screen door separating her from the overhanging deck. She stepped onto the decking, walking carefully over cracked and crumbling wood toward the jetty that stuck out into the bay.

The whirring sound grew louder, but Brooke could see no boat in sight. She raised her hand to her eyes to shield them from the bright blaze of the last crescent of sun sinking into the horizon.

It was then she saw a figure silhouetted against the orange ball. He was riding a Jet Ski, expertly streaking left, then right, across the bay at a terrifying speed, aiming straight for the deck . . . straight for her.

The engine revved with one final burst of speed before the Jet Ski sliced to a stop at the edge of the dock.

Instinct told Brooke she should leave while she had the chance. She turned toward the house, but stopped when the man disappeared under the water. All was quiet for a moment's heartbeat. Brooke held her breath, listening intently to the solitary sounds of lapping water hitting the dock, waiting, anticipating. . . .

Suddenly, like Neptune rising from the sea, he vaulted from the water. The splashing and roaring noise he created seemed louder and more ominous than that of the motor. Jumping onto the deck in front of her, he shook his head, sprinkling the area with cool droplets.

Brooke was strangely frozen to the spot. She tried to discern his features, but could not; the twilight sky behind him obscured his face. He didn't seem to see her as water ran off him in steady streams. He reached up and wiped his face. With his right hand, he slowly jerked down the zipper of his black, skintight wet suit. The sound ripped through the air as Brooke's gaze followed its descent.

It was then he noticed her. His hand stopped midway, and his lean body stiffened. He gave her a quick once-over, then visibly relaxed. A smile creased his face, and white teeth gleamed in the dusk. He acknowledged her presence with an almost imperceptible movement of his head.

Brooke swallowed and returned the nod. He seemed to be waiting for her to say something. She did not, could not. Her mouth was dry, her breathing irregular. If he was trying to frighten her, he was succeeding.

He took a step toward her, and instinctively Brooke retreated. He was very tall and loomed over her, looking like the devil himself shrouded in black against the amber sky. She hesitated when she thought she heard him laugh.

"Who are you?" she asked.

"Don't you remember me, Brooke?"

"How do you know my name?"

He took a step toward her. "I know a lot more than that about you, babe," he said softly.

Translucent blue eyes became visible, and her heart somersaulted.

No, not the devil.

But close.

"Devon."

He moved to her side. "Is that it? Just 'Devon'?"

"I—I'm surprised, that's all," she said, a hand to her chest attempting to still the triple beat of her heart. "It's been a long time."

"Fifteen years, give or take."

"You're back." She bit her tongue. Obviously.

His mouth turned up on one side, a half-smirk she remembered as his poor imitation of a smile. "In the flesh."

Yes, she thought.

Devon Taylor.

Her gaze fixed on his bare chest, the golden curls, freed from their constraints, glistening in the dusk.

In the flesh.

His hand moved up to wipe a line of water from his cheek. She followed the movement with her eyes until her gaze met his. Met and locked.

Fifteen years.

She shook her head as if to clear it, to return her senses back to reality. This was no stranger. This was Devon Taylor with whom she'd shared many of life's firsts...

Don't think of that.

She forced her mind blank and studied him. His tall frame was broader, and his blond-streaked hair shorter. She had nothing to fear from him...not any longer. That Devon had been dead and buried in her mind, in her heart, in her soul years ago.

"What brings you back?" she asked as casually as was possible.

"Do I need a reason?"

"Considering how you left, I'd say so."

He made a derisive sound. "Is that old news still being passed around? Hasn't Daddy ever run anybody else out of town?"

She stiffened. "Still blaming my father for your mistakes, Devon? Well, it's too late. Daddy died three years ago."

"I know."

The silence was thick and heavy between them.

"You could say you're sorry," she said.

His stare was hard, strange. "Yeah, I could."

She waited for him to continue, but instead his lips curled into that same half-grin.

He walked around her to the back door, swung it open, and held it for her. When she didn't move, he said, "Lighten up, Brooke. It's been a long time. Come on inside."

Brooke forced herself to take the first step. She didn't know what she was thinking, let alone how she was feeling. All she did know was that Devon Taylor was back, and the why of it hung heavily in her mind.

"The place is a mess," he said as he righted an overturned chair and pushed it in her direction. "Have a seat." He opened the refrigerator door. "I don't have much to offer. Beer or soda?"

"Soda's fine," she said.

He popped the lid and handed her a can of cola. She accepted it and, as if by rote, brought it to her lips. Brooke knew she should be asking him questions, but for the life of her, she couldn't think of a single one.

"Give me a minute to get out of this wet suit."

She nodded as he disappeared out of the room. An old-fashioned wind-up alarm clock sat on the kitchen counter. It had been her father's, and he seemed to be speaking to her through it, his words ticktocking in time to the beat of her heart. "Stay away from him, Brooke. Far away."

She hadn't listened to him then; she wasn't now. Sipping the cold soda, she swished it around in her mouth to rid herself of the taste of nervous fear.

Calm down, Brooke, she chided herself. You're a woman now, not a naive girl any longer. He has no power over you anymore.

It's Devon.

Only Devon.

His mind racing, Devon Taylor took the steps to the second-floor landing two at a time. He didn't even want to *speculate* about what it meant to have Brooke Pattersen sitting in his kitchen. She, and all she represented, conjured up visions that were better left buried if he was to accomplish what he'd come back to do.

At first he hadn't recognized her. Her hair was shorter, darker, and her figure fuller, more…womanly. It was hard to think of Brooke as a woman. The last time he'd seen her—well, he'd better not think of that night—but she had been reed-thin, more angles than curves.

Not so anymore.

By the time he entered the master bedroom, he was already half out of the wet suit. He tossed it into the tub in the connecting bathroom and grabbed a towel from the rack, then vigorously rubbed it through his hair.

He needed some time to gauge his reaction to her. It annoyed the hell out of him that he had reacted to her at all. He knew he would see her, of course, had planned it down to the last minute detail, but he hadn't counted on her showing up here at the house . . . at least not before he was ready for her.

Controlling his feelings about the inhabitants of Lenape Bay—particularly the Pattersens—was all part of his plan. He donned a sweat suit, then wrapped the damp towel around his neck as he combed his hair. Get control of yourself, man, he told his image in the mirror. After all, he couldn't afford to get sidetracked before he'd even begun, now could he?

What the hell was she doing here?

She couldn't have known he was coming back; no one did. The Realtor had assured him that both Brooke and Chuck were out of town. He'd purposely picked the end of the season when the beach would be deserted and the traffic down Dune Road at a minimum. He'd wanted a day or two to go over everything, get used to the place again before he showed his hand to the powers that be.

He tossed the towel onto the bed. All that had to change now. He'd have to contact Chuck tonight, no matter how late, to arrange the meeting for the first thing in the morning. If there was one thing he remembered about Lenape Bay, it was the efficiency of the grapevine. The seat of his kitchen chair wouldn't be cold before Brooke hit the phones. By morning everyone who was anyone would know Devon Taylor was back in town.

He grinned. A thrill of anticipation shot through him like a high-potency drug. This homecoming had been a long time in the making, and he wanted to savor each and every moment of it. If seeing Brooke sooner than later meant altering his plans a bit, so be it. He was flexible. Hell, he was more than flexible, he was ready for anything. He gave himself a quick once-over.

Anything at all.

Devon reappeared in the kitchen wearing a black-and-white warm-up suit. It was designer, and Brooke knew from her time living in Boston that it must have cost a small fortune. But then, he could afford it. She'd heard years ago that he'd struck it rich in the real-estate market of the eighties. It had more than surprised everyone in Lenape Bay. They'd always assumed the only kind of designer clothing Devon Taylor would ever wear would be prison stripes.

She studied him as he reached into the refrigerator for a beer. His thick golden hair was fashionably short, spiked and neatly combed back from his face. A face, Brooke noticed for the first time, that sported at least a day's worth of whiskers. She watched his Adam's apple bob up and down as he took a long drink.

"That's better," he said.

Brooke brought the soda can to her lips as she watched him over the rim. She needed to know why he'd come back, and what he was doing here in her family home. And she needed to do it without provoking him. She remembered him well enough to know that he would only tell you what he wanted you to know. There were too many issues between them, too many unanswered questions—questions that were perhaps better left as that. Her life was good now, whole and happy. She didn't want or need Devon Taylor disrupting it as she knew only too well he could.

"How have you been, Devon?" she asked.

He set the can on the cracked Formica counter and studied her for a moment as if he were trying to decide if her question was sincere. "Fine. I've been fine."

"We'd heard a few years ago that you were living in California. Are you still there?"

"I have a house there, yes. That's where my business is."

"Real estate, isn't it?"

He grinned. "You're pretty well informed."

Brooke moved her eyes from his. She remembered that unsettling ice-blue stare and how deeply it could penetrate. "You know small towns. We thrive on gossip."

"Especially about me," he said.

"You always did liven things up around here."

He took another swig of beer. "Ain't that the truth."

Brooke shifted in her seat. It was time to bite the bullet. "Why are you here, Devon? In this house, *my* house?"

Devon slowly wiped his mouth with the back of his hand as he casually leaned against the counter. "It's not your house anymore, Brooke." He paused for effect. "I bought the place."

Her heart slammed in her chest. Her stomach churned as her worst suspicion was confirmed.

"You . . ." She swallowed. "When?"

"Closed on it this morning. The Realtor signed the papers."

"I had no idea. Chuck never mentioned anyone was interested."

"Chuck doesn't know. The Realtor said he was in the city for the day. She said she was authorized to handle the transaction. Isn't that so?"

"Yes, but... When did you first look at the house?"

"When I was seven, Brooke. But I had to stay out on the road. I was never invited inside."

"Devon—"

"I looked this morning and bought this morning. I knew the house. I knew the owners. Wasn't much of a decision, now was it? Paid cash. You know me, babe."

Yes, she knew him. Impulsive. Arrogant. Trouble.

"So you haven't changed, have you, Devon?"

His blue eyes narrowed before he broke into a grin. "Oh, I've changed. You have no idea how much."

"Why are you here?"

He laughed and pushed away from the counter. "Nothing like getting right to the point, huh, Brooke?"

"You know me, Devon," she said, mimicking him.

"Yeah. Well, let's just say I was feeling nostalgic for the town. Coming back to my roots, and all."

"I don't believe that for a minute."

He raised his eyebrows and placed a hand, palm down, over his heart in mock horror. "You wound me, woman. Maybe I just wanted to see the old place again. What's so odd about that?"

"Nothing. But you could have rented a hotel room in town, not bought *my* family home if all you wanted was a walk down memory lane." She stood and placed her cola can in the sink. "How long is this visit planned for?"

"Did I say I was visiting?"

She turned to face him. As long as she could remember, his looks had taken her breath away. Golden hair, clear blue eyes, chiseled features. Perfect. Almost too perfect, saved perhaps by the tiniest of bumps on the bridge of his nose. She refused to dwell on how he'd come by that small imperfection....

"How long, Devon?" she repeated.

"What's it to you?"

"It's my business."

"Since when?"

"Since I was elected mayor."

Devon whistled. "Mayor, huh? The banker's daughter makes good. Must have made Daddy happy as a clam."

The barb hurt. He knew, better than anyone perhaps, how she'd always struggled to please her father. Once she would have shed tears over his remark, but those days were long gone. Small hurts were easily ignored; handling the big ones had made her tough.

"How long?" she said, refusing to be put off.

He shrugged. "I don't know. It depends."

"On what?"

"On how bad Lenape Bay wants me to stay."

Brooke stared at him. She knew he wanted her to ask what he meant by that. He had to know there wasn't a soul in town who would welcome him back with open arms, even after all this time.

"If that's the case, it should be a short trip."

Devon finished the last of the beer and crushed the can. "Maybe, maybe not," he said with a smile. "Times change. So do people. You never know."

He threw the crushed can, basketball style, into the trash in the corner. Brooke walked over and gingerly picked it out. She dangled it in front of him by her thumb and index finger.

"In Lenape Bay, we recycle, Mr. Taylor."

Devon took the can from her. "I'll remember that, Mayor Pattersen."

"Wallace. Mayor Wallace."

"Married, Brooke?"

"Divorced, Devon."

"Ah." He caught her hand, and brushed a quick kiss across her knuckles. "I'll remember that, too."

She pulled her hand away, and wiped the spot he had kissed. "Some memories are better left as just that."

She walked to the front door. Devon held open the battered screen. "I agree. I have no interest in what was, only in what is."

Brooke stopped on the porch step. It was pitch dark now, except for the pale glow of the moon. Though she needed to get away from him so that she could sort through her feelings, she turned to look at him one last time.

"When are you going to tell me what you're up to?" she asked.

He smiled a devastating toothpaste-commercial smile. "Sooner than you think." The screen door snapped shut. "Sweet dreams, Mayor Wallace."

He disappeared inside, leaving her with moonlight and memories too potent to ignore.

Two

Brooke's dreams that night were anything but sweet. They were filled with dark figures encased in the sinister glare of headlights, visible but not clear, yet she instinctively knew who they were and where they were.

Chuck and Devon. Midnight. Main Street. Her father's bank. Shouting. Her own voice, screaming. The sickening sound of bare fists connecting with flesh. Devon swinging, Chuck spinning in the air...

Chuck's battered face cradled in her lap, her once pristine-white prom gown bloodied, torn and soiled beyond repair. The sound of a car engine turning over...Devon behind the wheel of her father's old gray Cadillac, gunning the engine, spewing up a blast of choking exhaust and gravel....

Devon's eyes shone in the dark like iridescent jewels. She tried to run to him, to stop him from what he was about to do, but something held her back—Chuck, his arms tight like bands around her middle.

Helplessly, struggling to be free, her eyes held Devon's across the space of only a few feet but what might as well have been miles. She was screaming at him, crying, begging, ranting, raving, all to no avail. He released the brake, and the car careened forward at a horrific speed, its back wheels screeching in protest as he crashed through the floor-to-ceiling front window of Pattersen Central Bank.

The impact sent her falling onto the hard, concrete sidewalk as the window ruptured, sending shards of shattered glass cascading all over them. In that split second of silence before the bank alarm sounded, Brooke wondered if Devon was dead, so still was his body slumped over the wheel. Then all hell broke loose as the siren went off at ear-splitting volume.

She covered her ears with her hands. Devon emerged from the car, his white tuxedo shirt sprinkled with slivers of glass, his face bloody but triumphant, his eyes as intense as an efficient blue flame.

He came to her and held out his hand.

"Come with me, Brooke."

She reached up and put her hand in his....

He took her to the cabin, their own special place on the beach. It had been deserted years before and was falling apart from neglect, but Devon had found it and had made it their perfect hideaway, away from prying eyes and Daddy's rules.

Devon's mood was wild...crazy...and she was caught up in it. The fight with Chuck had exhilarated him. His clear blue gaze froze her to the spot as he trailed a finger down her bare arm. She reached for him, and he wasted no time in pulling her into his arms, kissing her so deeply he seemed to reach her soul. The feel of his skin on hers, the taste of his mouth, and the powerful heat of his body touched off a long-repressed spark of desire. It was all that was needed to ignite the power and passion of their young love.

Devon undressed her slowly, with such tenderness, the harshness of the earlier violence evaporated into the night air. He touched her hair, her face, her breasts, belly, and below, where only he had ever touched her. She became a woman that night...his woman...as they made love for the first time on the hardwood floor of the cabin. Every touch, every caress, every sensation was magnified tenfold as he joined his body to hers. It had been everything she'd ever dreamed it would be, and her heart had filled to bursting with love for him—

Brooke awoke at that moment, as if some internal defense mechanism had automatically kicked in, protecting her from reliving the rest. Heart pounding, she threw her legs over the side of the bed and wrapped a terry robe around her before heading out onto the porch.

It was very late. The moon was still high overhead with no hint of dawn in sight. It cast a yellow stream of light across the ripples on the bay. Brooke sank into the soft cushions of her rattan rocker, a leg tucked under her. She swayed back and forth to a slow inner rhythm as she gazed out between the slats of the jalousie windows. A light breeze drifted in. The air was sweet with the smell of the sea.

Outside, all was quiet, lazy and calm. Inside, the opposite was true. Her mind was traveling at warp speed, bouncing back and forth through kaleidoscope images from the past.

It had been years since she'd had that dream. During college, it had come frequently, almost to the point where she'd anticipate it, particularly after a date with someone new. It had seemed as if Devon hovered nearby, ready and able to reassert his claim on her...as if his spirit lurked somewhere in the shadows, possessive, jealous, watching to be sure that no one else ever became special in her life . . . as if even though he didn't want her, he would make sure no one else could have her.

It had been all in her mind, of course. She had never heard from Devon after that night. It had haunted her for years, the whys and wherefores of an experience that could only be described as a splendid nightmare.

For too many years she'd second-guessed herself as to why she'd left with him after he demolished her father's car and bank. Like a love-struck fool, she'd followed him to that dilapidated cabin on the beach where she'd defied Chaz's strictest orders. It was the first and last time in her life she had ever openly disobeyed her father, but at the time there was no rhyme or reason to her actions: she was hopelessly, irrevocably in love.

Brooke rose and walked into the living room. She poured herself a glass of Chardonnay and took a sip of the cool, fruity liquid as she stared out over the bay. That night was the last time she'd laid eyes on Devon Taylor until today. It wasn't supposed to be that way, of course. They were supposed to spend a lifetime together. She shook her head, but refused to allow the lump in her throat to grow into something more. She'd cried a sea of tears over him, and swore long ago that she would shed no more.

Brooke carried the wineglass to the kitchen and made her way back to the bedroom. She wanted more than anything to fall into bed and oblivion, but her mind refused to rest, and she knew she had to see it through to the end, relive all of it, if she was ever going to sleep another wink this night.

She sat on the edge of the bed and ran her fingers through her hair, lifting it off her neck as she rolled her head from side to side, allowing her thoughts to travel back in time.

Long after they'd made love, Devon had held her in his arms. They'd whispered words of love to each other and promises that would never be kept. He had to leave town, and she had agreed. There was no way her father wouldn't press charges against him after what he'd done to the bank. He told her he loved her, asked her to marry him. With stars in her eyes, she'd said yes, and they made plans to meet at the cabin in the morning.

He drove her back to the bay and dropped her down the road from her house. Dawn was just starting to break over the horizon, and she knew the trouble she'd face if she crossed paths with Chuck or her father. She planned to sneak into the house, collect her things and escape before they saw her.

Brooke grinned at her own naiveté. To think that she, at seventeen, was any match for Chaz Pattersen had been a delusion of the grandest order, but she had indeed thought to slip in and out of the house unnoticed. Such was not the case of course. Chaz was waiting for her, more livid than she had ever seen him in his life. It was the first time she was ever truly frightened of her father.

The local police chief had questioned her until after the sun rose high in the sky, but she never told him a thing about Devon's plan. When they'd finally let her go, she ran upstairs and packed her things, but Chaz and Chuck were gone and so were both cars. Stranded but not defeated, she walked the few miles, taking a shortcut through the dunes to reach the beach. But by the time she arrived at the cabin, Devon was gone. She'd waited for him, unbelieving that he would have left without her. By dusk, she had given up and traipsed back home, dragging her suitcase behind her. Something had happened, she'd rationalized. She was sure he would return, or at least send a message. But he had not.

Not then, not ever.

Brooke hadn't been able to ask her father about Devon, and Chuck claimed he knew nothing. She'd tried to approach his mother, but Mrs. Taylor had quit working for her family when Devon left town. The woman had refused to speak to Brooke and had all but slammed the door in her face. In September, she'd had no choice but to go on to college on the scholarship she'd won. When Devon's mother put the house up for sale and moved away, it seemed a dead issue.

Devon never called, never wrote, and the pain had cut deep into her soul. Chuck had taunted her as brothers tend to do, reminding her that once "he'd got what he wanted," Devon took off for greener pastures. Chuck called him a coward, and though her heart didn't want to believe her brother, reality was hard to ignore.

A word here or there trickled back to town from time to time—someone who knew someone who had run into Devon over the years, but that was all. No direct communication of any kind.

Until now.

What did he want? she wondered. Why was he back? Surely not to rekindle anything between the two of them. He'd killed whatever feelings she'd had for him years ago. For the longest time she'd actually hated him, but no more. She didn't love him; she didn't hate him. She didn't know what she felt about him.

The only thing she knew for sure was that she didn't trust him.

Brooke glanced at the telephone on the night table. The moment she'd walked through the door, her first thought had been to call Chuck, but if he hadn't returned from the city, she'd have to leave a message with his wife. She preferred not to deal with Lotty unless it was absolutely necessary. An extremely efficient housewife, Lotty was a bit too prissy for Brooke's taste. Over the years she and Brooke had drifted into a separate-but-equal relationship.

She could try to reach Chuck in the city, she supposed, but deep down she knew that Devon expected her to do just that, and as much as she resented that fact, it also stopped her cold.

Once again she wished her father were still alive, yet she wondered what even he could do in this situation. Chaz had always known how to handle trouble, but the Taylors had stumped him, too. They were rebels, and Chaz's conservative banker's mind could not tolerate what he'd called "their type." Jack Taylor had defied Chaz by taking his banking business elsewhere, and it had always stuck in Chaz's craw.

After Jack's death, all Chaz's animosity became centered around Devon. No one else in town had been able to arouse her father's ire the way Devon had. When Devon was young, Chaz had simply "disapproved" of him, not allowing either of his children to associate with the boy, but by the time high school rolled around, Chaz was openly hostile. The fact that Mrs. Taylor cleaned house for them only seemed to acerbate the situation.

Perhaps Chaz had sensed Devon's interest in Brooke long before it had ever manifested itself. She didn't know, but by her senior year, their budding relationship was a potboiler issue in the Pattersen household, one she should have realized was destined to come to a violent end.

Brooke had always been more sensitive to the hurts Devon endured from her father and the town. She'd never had the nerve to tell Devon, but she had seen his wildness for the anger that it was. She never knew exactly what had triggered it, but things had gone from bad to worse in the months after Devon's father was killed in a car accident and his construction business lost.

Devon became impossible then, breaking all the rules as he and his motorcycle became a source of irritation for the entire town. It didn't take a genius to know that he, she, and her father were on a collision course; it was just a matter of when.

Brooke squeezed her eyes shut and sighed. She wouldn't think about it anymore now. Her emotions were on overload with the dredging up of unsettling memories. She rechecked the alarm. She needed to get up early in the morning to contact Chuck before he left for the bank.

Satisfied that all was in order, she yanked up the comforter and wrapped herself in a cocoon. In the split second before sleep took her, she made a mental note to dress up for the office tomorrow.

Without a doubt, it was going to be a very interesting day.

Devon surveyed the conference room at Pattersen Central Bank. He was alone, seated at the head of a large, rectangular mahogany table. The air-conditioning provided the usual background "white noise," and the sun streamed in the windows through neutral vertical blinds.

He remembered the last time he was in this room. He hadn't been invited to sit that day, least of all in the chair at the head of the table. No, that chair was reserved for one man only, and that was the president, Chaz Pattersen.

It had been February, a freezing, bone-cold day, but as Devon had stood in front of Chaz, the sweat had rolled down his back. He remembered the fear he'd felt confronting the older man, literally hat in hand, asking for a loan to save his late father's business. More than that, he remembered the humiliation at having to come crawling to Pattersen, something he knew his father would never, ever have done, no matter how bad things had become.

But Jack Taylor had died in a car crash six months before, and Taylor Construction was going under fast. His mother had tried her best to keep the business going, but their customers were reluctant to do business with her and a nineteen-year-old boy, and so they lost contract after contract, until they could no longer pay the bills on the equipment.

The bank that held the business loans was about to foreclose, and Devon swore he would do everything and anything to stop that from happening...even if it meant humbling himself before the godlike Chaz Pattersen.

It had been a joke, he realized now, to even imagine Chaz being so generous as to help anyone in that situation, but especially him, especially Jack Taylor's son. Chaz and Jack had had a falling-out years before when Jack, fed up with Chaz's high-handedness, had moved his business to another bank in a neighboring town. Chaz hated losing control of anything in Lenape Bay, and the fact that Taylor Construction flourished during those years had been a major thorn in his side.

Knowing all that, Devon had still been cocky enough to approach Chaz for help. No one had been more surprised than he when Chaz approved the loan, using a second mortgage on their family home as collateral. Chaz had even offered his mother a job taking care of his big house on the bay. It had seemed the solution to all their problems.

Devon winced at his own gullibility. That money immediately went to pay for the equipment, but he soon found that he couldn't run the business without more money to buy material and pay the workers.

Of course, Chaz had known that all along, and rejected any further loans on the basis that the Taylors had no more collateral. Everything had to be sold off, and the company folded. When all was said and done, they were penniless. But that was not the worst part. The worst part was that Chaz Pattersen not only employed his mother, he held their mortgage, as well. He had both Taylors right where he'd always wanted them—in the palm of his hand.

Devon had sworn then that he would get back at Chaz for how he'd taken advantage and manipulated them. At nineteen, however, his opportunities for doing damage to Pattersen Central Bank were limited to say the least. He did find one way to get back at Chaz, however, and that was on a purely personal level.

Devon had methodically and relentlessly pursued the apple of Chaz's eye and Lenape Bay's All-American girl. It had worked, too. Until it backfired.

Chuck Pattersen entered the room, followed by a group of men. As Chuck introduced them, each nodded their response as they assembled around the conference table. One or two familiar faces came up to shake his hand and exchange pleasantries, but for the most part, the businessmen of Lenape Bay were reluctant to approach him until they heard what he had to say.

Devon checked his watch. It was five after eight in the morning, and he was alert, wide-eyed and ready for action. The ambivalent group before him looked anything but. It was one of the reasons he had asked for such a meeting. He'd learned a long time ago that the early bird had a distinct advantage. Over the years he had conditioned himself to rise at dawn, swim before showering, and imbibe a healthy dose of caffeine to get his motor off and running.

He watched and waited as the coffee thermos was passed around. Occasionally someone would catch his eye, and he'd smile and nod in reply. He'd expected the curious looks, but found himself enjoying the ones of trepidation, as well. They were scared; that was good. The more scared they were, the easier it would be.

It had been a long time since he'd seen the men in this room. There were one or two new faces, but for the most part, the town council—minus the late, great Chaz Pattersen—still consisted of the ten or so men who had virtually run Lenape Bay since the day he was born.

He glanced across the table at Chuck Pattersen and told himself he would have to do. When Devon had learned of Chaz's death, it had stung him as numb as if he'd fallen headfirst into a wasp nest. All his schemes and plans had been aimed at Chaz, and to have the man up and die on him seemed more than unfair. It had depressed him, and it had taken him a long time to decide what to do. Yet no matter how much he mulled over it all, one fact remained the same: each and every Pattersen had a part in what had happened to his family, and each would have to pay.

Chuck grinned at him. Devon studied Chuck's receding hairline and paunch. The man had even started to look like old Chaz. Devon returned the smile.

Yes, he'll do nicely.

Enough of the past. He checked his watch. Brooke was late. He hadn't invited her, but he had been sure she'd find out about the meeting in advance. Too bad. It was time to begin.

"Gentlemen," Devon said. "I'm sure you're all wondering why I've returned to Lenape Bay." He smiled and acknowledged the affirmative nods. "Well, I'm here because I have—"

"Excuse me? Mr. Pattersen?" Chuck's secretary stuck her head in the door.

"What is it, Barbara?"

"It's Mayor Wallace. She wants to, uh, come in? Is that all right?"

Chuck Pattersen looked over at Devon.

"By all means," Devon said.

The door swung open, and Brooke walked inside. Her eyes scanned the room, then settled on Devon.

"I'm sorry to interrupt, but I'd like to sit in, if you don't mind?"

Brooke ignored her brother and addressed Devon. Sitting at the head of the table, there wasn't a doubt in her mind that he was running the show.

When she'd awakened this morning, the air around her had seemed charged. With sleep still clouding her brain, it had taken a minute for her to pinpoint the source of the electricity, but then it slammed into her with the force of a fist.

Devon was back.

She'd jumped out of bed and quickly showered. Gulping a half cup of coffee, she'd made an early morning attempt to contact Chuck, but Lotty had said he'd gone already. Gone to a town council meeting at the bank. She'd thanked Lotty and hung up, secure in the knowledge that whatever Devon was up to, he was one, possibly two steps ahead of her and everyone else in town.

With speed and energy she hadn't had in years, Brooke had dressed and sped down Dune Road into town, hoping to make the meeting. If the amused look in Devon's eyes was any indication, she shouldn't have rushed so. He glanced at the chair on his left...as if he'd purposely left it empty for her.

Devon watched a gamut of emotions cross over her face. She looked sensational. Last night she'd seemed tired, washed out, and the shock of her arrival had taken him by surprise. He'd been too concerned about why she'd come to notice much about how she looked. But the bright light of day accentuated her hazel eyes, the honey highlights in her chestnut hair, and the creaminess of her complexion.

She was dressed in a soft gray pin-striped suit with a stark white blouse and a skirt that was just a trifle short. The outfit was very businesslike and very professional, but it also fit perfectly, showing off each and every curve as well as her long, shapely legs.

He'd forgotten about those legs. A flash of them— tanned, bare, and tightly wrapped around his waist— shot through his mind.

Devon stared a moment too long. He knew it the second he raised his eyes to the rest of the group, which seemed inordinately anxious for him to continue. He took a sip of water while Brooke made her way around the table to take the only vacant seat on his left.

Devon scanned the group. He cleared his throat to rid himself of what he wasn't sure. "As I was saying…" He opened his briefcase, lifted out several folders and passed them around the table. "I have a proposition for your consideration. If you will take a moment to look over the first page of the packet you've just been given, you will see that my proposal involves a piece of prime real estate just north of town on Maiden Point."

"That's the abandoned Richards' condo-tel project," Mr. Antonelli said. He owned two of the town's bakeries, and Devon knew for a fact that he'd lost a pretty penny when the combination condominium and hotel project went belly-up.

"Yes," Devon said. "We're interested in taking it over and completing it."

A murmur ran through the group as the impact of Devon's proposal took effect.

"'We'? Who's 'we'?" Chuck asked.

"A consortium of investors that I've put together over the years. We are always on the lookout for good opportunities, and in recent years, with the slump in the real-estate market, it has become beneficial for us to buy up foreclosed properties and revamp or complete the job that had been started. The Maiden Point project fits this criteria perfectly."

"But it went bankrupt in the first place because there were no buyers. The market is still dead. How do you plan to sell the finished units?" one of the men asked.

"Good question," Devon said. "And the answer is quite simple. Price. Since the project continues to put a strain on Chuck's bank, I'm sure he'd let it go for a song. Right, Chuck?"

All eyes turned to Chuck Pattersen, and Brooke's heart clenched. She loved her brother despite their differences, but that didn't mean she ignored his weaknesses. Though no one ever said it out loud, everyone agreed he was a shadow of the man his father had been. Chuck was most assuredly out of his depth. His years as a football hero, coupled with his mediocre college career, did nothing to ready him for such a task. The bank—and the town along with it—had suffered from his inept management.

"Well, I don't know," Chuck said. "We'll have to discuss that, Devon."

"Of course. And I'll be available to each and every one of you to answer your specific questions," Devon said. "But I have done my homework, Chuck. My records show that each month Pattersen Central holds onto that property, money is lost. I'd think you'd be willing to do anything to have an investment group come in and take it off your hands."

"Now wait a minute—"

"No, you wait." The folder landed on the table with a thwack. "You're in trouble." He looked up at the group of businessmen assembled before him. "You're *all* in trouble. Lenape Bay is dying, slowly but surely, as is every other town in the area." Devon leaned back from the table. "It is very clear that business is off more than thirty percent in the last season alone. How much longer can you all go on like this? This project is going to bring three hundred *new* families a week into the area each and every week of the season. We'll attract a whole new generation of people. Lenape Bay needs to update itself, and Maiden Point is the first step."

The group began to talk among themselves. Devon studied each face, stopping short at Brooke's. She wasn't involved in the conversations going on around her. She was studying him.

"What's this going to cost me?" Chuck Pattersen asked.

Devon turned to him. "A lot, but all reinvestment will go through this bank. All mortgages will go through this bank, and all renovation loans will go through this bank. In other words, initially you take all the risks, but in the long run, you reap all the rewards."

Chuck's eyes lit up, and Devon could almost see the dollar signs dancing in his head. For the first time, he offered up a prayer of thanks that the Lord had seen fit to call Chaz into the great beyond. As much as Devon had hated the old man, he had also respected his shrewd and cunning mind. Fortunately Chuck had inherited none of it.

Brooke watched as Devon grinned, seemingly unable to hold back his satisfaction a minute longer. She glanced at the other men around the table, and couldn't believe what she was seeing. These men, for the most part, had never failed to hide their distaste for the rebellious Devon. They had been willing to see him go to jail, or worse, if it had been legally possible, and now they sat here, foaming at the mouth, falling all over themselves at his offer to pull them out of their financial difficulties.

She studied him, consumed with a desire to jump into his head, to discover what he was really up to. She didn't believe for a minute that he was doing this out of the goodness of his heart.

"I have a question," Brooke said.

Everyone stopped shuffling and turned to her.

"Please," Devon said, extending his hand, palm-up, in her direction.

"I'd like to know what's in this for you, Devon."

"That's simple, Brooke. Money."

"That's it? Just money?"

"I think that's a perfectly good reason," Devon said as he looked around the room. "Don't you?"

"Okay, then," she said, "I'll rephrase my question." She leaned an elbow on the table and rested her chin in her palm. "Why here, Devon? Why us?"

The room became still and Devon's face turned very serious. All watched him intently, but none more so than Brooke.

It started in his eyes. The watercolor blue turned warm and vibrant, and slowly, the corners crinkled a precious moment before his mouth turned up in a slow, seductive smile.

"I think that should be the most obvious of all. This is home. Always has been, always will be."

She tilted her head and raised her eyebrows. "Excuse me for being cynical, Devon, but didn't you leave *home* under less than auspicious circumstances?"

He laughed out loud. "You're something, you really are! I think everyone here knows or has heard that old story, but as far as I'm concerned, that's all water under the bridge. I was a kid, and I'll admit, I was wrong. If you want an apology, then you have it. I'm officially sorry for all the hell I raised in town all those years ago."

He turned from Brooke to look over the group. "But as you can see, I've changed. I want to do something good for this town. I don't know, maybe in return for all the bad. I want to fix up the old Pattersen house, move my mother back here to live so that she can be with her old friends. And, yes, maybe make her just a little bit proud of me."

He stood. "That's what this project means to me. Don't decide now. Look over the plan and check it out. I want each of you to be one hundred percent behind this. I'm certain once you study it, you'll agree it's a good deal for all of us. I hope you'll give me the opportunity to prove it."

The applause stunned her, almost as much as the sight of these grown men fighting each other to get to Devon to shake his hand. If she'd had a handkerchief, she would have dabbed at her eyes, so wrought with emotion was his little speech. She tried to study his face over the group, but he was good-naturedly taking the thanks and congratulations from the men with the same sincere "aw shucks" attitude from before.

And she didn't believe him. Not for a minute.

She sat back and waited as he shook the last hand, slapped the last back. She waited still as he stood talking to Chuck, ironing out some of the finer points, making appointments to further discuss the mechanics of such a project.

Every now and then, he looked her way, telling her with his eyes and the slightest turn of his head that he knew what she was thinking. It irked her that he seemed amused by it all. As she watched the rest of the group file out, words of praise dripping from their lips, she shook her head.

She felt like Dorothy in the land of Oz.

"Okay, Mayor. Spit it out," Devon said when the last man left the room.

"I don't know what you want me to say," she said.

"From the look on your face, I'd say it was some profound phrase that starts with a *B* and ends with a *T*."

"Am I that transparent?"

"To me, babe."

She stared at him. "I don't get it, Devon. You hate us. I know you do."

He shook his head. "Not anymore. Oh, I'll admit I used to. I'd spend half my day hating each and every citizen of Lenape Bay. The other half, I'd feel sorry for myself. But you know something? That gets real old, real quick. It's over, Brooke. Cross my heart," he said, and did.

The childhood gesture got to her the way no words before could. He seemed sincere, and she wanted to believe him so much it hurt. She looked into those fabulous blue eyes and shivered inwardly. It frightened her to realize how much she needed to believe he was the one who would come to their rescue, save the town. A more unlikely guardian angel they couldn't have imagined in their wildest dreams.

But if he was the one, *truly* the one who could help them, she'd be a fool to let old hurts and suspicions stand in the way.

"Okay, Devon. I'll keep an open mind."

"That's all I ask," he said.

Brooke smiled, the first sincere smile she'd given him since he'd arrived. He returned the grin and extended his hand. She accepted it, and she felt the dry warmth penetrate deep into her skin.

"Just give me the chance, Brooke. You'll see. I promise. I'll show you all," Devon said.

He squeezed her hand tighter, ignoring the good, warm feelings that seeped into his soul. There was no place for them now.

I'll show you all.

Three

———

The air was cool, the water warm. Devon gunned the engine of the Jet Ski and swept out toward the middle of the bay. The sun was low in the sky, obscured by a smidgen of cloud cover, and he headed straight for the muted light.

This was his favorite time of day on the bay. As a kid, he'd sneak down here and sit on the dock to watch the sun set, skipping broken clam shells across the water and dreaming little-boy dreams of being grown up, of being able to do anything he wanted to do, anytime.

Some of his best memories of Lenape Bay took place right here, away from town, away from the teachers, shopkeepers and just regular *people* who had made his life so miserable. This place represented freedom, and even now that he *was* that grown-up who could do anything he wanted anytime, he found that what he wanted most of all was the peace of mind he'd felt sitting on the dock.

He veered off to the left around a buoy, riding farther out into the center of the bay. Would he behave differently now if he had the chance to do it all over again? He doubted it. There was something inside him, something that no one seemed to understand. It was an energy that drove him to do things his way. He'd never understood why everyone always wanted him to conform to *their* way, when *his* way worked so well.

Since leaving Lenape Bay, he'd proved it in many ways, but none as spectacularly as in his real-estate career where he'd bought up properties the experts told him were worthless and had turned them into pure gold.

Devon smiled, lifting his face to the force of the wind and the spray of the water. His mother always said his epithet should read "Don't tell me what to do!" And she was right. There was no more sure-fire way to get him to act on something than to tell him he couldn't do it.

He made a wide turn and headed south. The Jet Ski bounced so hard into the waves, he had to hang on tightly so as not to lose control. He loved speed, always had. Be it on land, air or sea, it gave him a feeling of power like no other. It also forced him to concentrate so hard on the challenge at hand that all stress and strain was automatically drained from his mind.

It had been a very long day. He'd been on a high ever since the meeting this morning. He had made himself available throughout the day to answer specific questions posed by members of the council. When he'd returned to the house, the phone hadn't stopped ringing with inquiries from others interested in what he'd had to say.

All in all, it had gone well—better, in fact, than he had expected. Chuck Pattersen had grown to his full potential as village idiot in much the way Devon had imagined. The old football hero airhead was now a bank president airhead. Devon wondered if old Chaz was sitting up—or, better yet, *down*—somewhere watching this whole charade, shaking his head, pounding his fist, and getting red in the face. That would be true justice, but fate had taken that ace out of his hand. Devon had reconciled himself to the fact that Chaz was being paid back by someone infinitely more powerful and righteous than he.

The wind was picking up, and Devon decided it was time to head back. He checked the shoreline and realized that he'd ridden past his house down toward the bay's head. It was almost dark now, but he could see the lights of a cottage on the thin inlet that looked out into the bay. The red convertible in the driveway told him it was Brooke's place.

He slowed the engine, weighing the wisdom of a surprise visit. Mayor Brooke Wallace was definitely part of his plan, perhaps even the focal point of it. He thought of the meeting this morning. She'd grown into old Chaz's daughter, all right, complete with the condescending look and cool air of superiority. Funny, he'd never noticed it while they were growing up—he, who always knew it all. Funnier still that he had fallen so hard for her that he had been too blind to see past her lies. Funniest of all was how she'd shown her true colors in the end.

When he'd first asked her on a date, his only purpose had been to spite Chaz. He knew Brooke, but they didn't exactly travel in the same circles. She was the All-American girl, the head cheerleader, the scholarship winner who was going to conquer the world. He was the son of a construction worker who came from the wrong side of the tracks. Her strict upbringing had made her too uptight for his tastes.

Even so, he wasn't surprised when she said yes when he asked her out. Though he wasn't the star athlete or country-club type, girls fell over themselves to go out with him. He wasn't conceited, but knew it was his looks as much as his aura of danger that attracted them, and he used both to his advantage. At first Brooke was just a means to an end, another girl just like all the rest . . . but then his plan backfired.

He fell in love.

Her sweetness and caring nature were too much even for the young, cynical Devon to fight. She had broken through his shell, reached deep inside and saw things that others wouldn't, couldn't see. She had been the only one in the world, other than his parents, that he'd ever trusted with his secret thoughts and inner feelings. He would have never believed that she could do what she did to him.

A spray of water slapped Devon's face. With crystal clarity he could still remember that morning after the prom as he sat pathetically on the floor of the cottage, on the exact spot where they'd made love the night before. His overflowing knapsack had rested between his legs as he waited impatiently for Brooke to show up. His mind had been filled with plans for the two of them, so much so that he'd never heard the cars pull up.

Sunlight had just been beginning to break overhead when the cottage door slammed open, framing the massive form of Chaz Pattersen. The hate in the older man's eyes had been potent, but not half as threatening as the baseball bat in his hand. When Chuck's battered face had appeared in the doorway behind Chaz, Devon had thought he was a goner for sure.

But Chaz never used the bat, never had to. He'd stood in front of him, legs spread, slapping the thick round bat against the palm of his left hand as he spoke, so softly, if Devon hadn't known better, he'd think he was in church.

"This is the end of the line, boy, the very end. You've got one hour to get yourself out of Lenape Bay, or I'll have your butt in jail so fast your pretty-boy head'll be spinning."

"Don't waste your breath," Devon had answered, heart pounding, but eyes as cold as ice. "My bag is packed. I'm on my way. But I'm not going alone."

Chaz's eyes had narrowed for a long moment before a huge grin spread across his face. "You think so?"

"I know so."

Chuck had made a derisive sound at that and lunged forward to attack Devon, but Chaz motioned him back.

"And who do you think you're taking with you?"

"You know exactly who. And she'll be here any minute," Devon had said.

"Don't count on it."

"She'll be here."

Chaz had laughed then, out loud. "If you think that, Taylor, you're not as smart as I gave you credit . . . and you sure as hell don't know a lot about women."

"What do you mean?"

"I mean, boy . . . how do you think I found you? How'd I know to come here to this cabin? How'd I know you'd be here? Ever think of that?"

Devon had swallowed, his throat closing rapidly with each successive word Chaz had uttered.

"No answer, smart boy? Well, I'll tell you anyway. Brooke told me all about last night...all of it. She's seventeen. For that alone, I could put you away, but I'm in a magnanimous mood this morning, and I'm going to let you go."

"I don't believe you."

"No? Then you sit here, and you wait, and you'll see what happens. She's not going to show, boy, and that's a fact. Did you really think she'd give up her scholarship to traipse around the country with a loser like you?"

"Brooke loves me, and I love her."

"Brooke had a fling, an experiment, and now she'll go on with her life just as we planned it...without you."

"Maybe I won't leave."

"Oh, you'll leave all right. Today in fact. Or your mama'll pay the price."

"Keep my mother out of this."

"Can't do that. She not only works for me, I hold the mortgage on that house of hers. Did you forget how you handed that to me on a silver platter?" His belly bounced as he laughed. "And it won't take me two minutes to put the papers together to call it in. Don't believe me? Try me, Taylor, just try me, and she'll be out on the street before the leaves fall off the trees."

"You bastard."

"It takes one to know one, boy, it takes one to know one." Chaz had motioned to Chuck to leave. "Don't be here when I get back, Devon. It won't be so pleasant next time." Chaz had stopped at the doorway and turned. "And another thing. I don't want to see your face ever again."

Devon swung the Jet Ski to the right and made a beeline for the shore. Chaz never did see his face ever again, so the old man had gotten his wish. Devon had waited that morning, long past the time Brooke was supposed to arrive. It had been the longest wait of his life as he'd sat there in the middle of the room, the sun filtering through the windows until it was full up.

He'd been a stubborn cuss, though. Even then, he buzzed passed her house on his motorcycle on his way out of town. Chuck had been standing outside ready to do battle once again. Devon had revved the engine to alert Brooke to his presence, ignoring Chuck's taunts that Brooke wanted no part of him. He'd almost jumped off the motorcycle and lunged for Chuck when his peripheral vision caught the movement of curtains in Brooke's upstairs bedroom window. When he looked up, she jumped back, the curtain swaying into place.

Devon still remembered the knot in his stomach twisting his insides, turning him to stone. He'd left town with a lump in his throat and a hollow spot in his heart. Pride had stopped him from coming back. Once, months after, when he'd had too much to drink, he'd called her around midnight, but Chaz had answered the phone, and he'd hung up.

Brooke's betrayal had been the bitterest pill he'd ever had to swallow, and the hollow spot in his soul had never truly healed. There had been women in his life, to be sure, but no one had reached as deep as Brooke. He'd filled the spot with hate instead, and a need for vengeance so intense that it had pushed him all these years, kept him going, centered, with his eyes on the ultimate prize: the destruction of each and every Pattersen.

Devon cut the engine and coasted. He sank in the water, then pulled himself onto Brooke's dock. He had mixed feelings about seeing her here. Better to deal with her in her office, better to deal with her as Mayor Wallace rather than Brooke. She was suspicious of him, and that did not bode well. He needed her, perhaps more than anyone, on his side. Convincing her of his sincerity was going to be an uphill battle to say the least. But then, there was nothing Devon liked more than a challenge.

He stood and shook himself off. The wind chilled him, and he knew he'd have to make a quick decision to stay or move on. He couldn't very well stand here all night staring at the light coming from the cottage, trying to make up his mind what he wanted more: seeing Brooke or staying safe.

True to form, Devon tied the Jet Ski to the dock and made his way to her back door.

Brooke cradled the telephone, contemplatively tapping her fingers against the receiver as she stared into space. She had just hung up with Chuck, doing her best to get answers to her questions about Devon and his project.

The town was buzzing. She had not seen this much activity since the centennial celebration three years ago. She hated to admit it, but Devon's arrival had infused the town with something that it hadn't had in years: hope. As reluctant as she was to give her full support to this project, she couldn't deny that it was the shot in the arm they needed to get moving.

News traveled quickly, and by afternoon she'd fielded calls from three other bay town mayors looking for information about Maiden Point. They wanted to know if Lenape Bay had approved the plan, and if not, could she give them the name of the developer. Each had a prime piece of land that was tailor-made for Devon's project.

A feeding frenzy was taking place among the area's newspapers, and rumors were flying fast and furious. She'd spent most of her day trying to separate the truth from fiction, leaving precious little time to delve into Devon's proposal and judge its merits.

It seemed that no one but her cared about that. Everyone she spoke to today discussed the project as if it were a done deal. Not one businessman had taken the time to make some phone calls to check out Devon's list of investors, or even to check with the other projects Devon had used as role models for Maiden Point.

She knew it wasn't her place to do this. This was up to Chuck and the council, but she wasn't about to sit by and let them commit the town to what could just as easily be a monumental mistake as it was a godsend.

Time was what she needed. Given a month or so, she and her assistant could track down the information needed to make an educated decision. All she needed to do now was convince Chuck and the town council to calm down, take it slow, and approach this thing with level heads.

That, she was afraid, was easier said than done.

Brooke turned at the sound of her patio screen door rattling open. Hand on heart, she relaxed when she saw it was Devon.

"You scared the life out of me!" she said as she pulled on the storm door to admit him. A blast of cool air hit her, and she shut it just as quickly.

"Sorry," he said. "I saw the light, and thought I'd drop in. If you're busy—"

"No, no. Come on in." She looked at his wet suit. "You must be freezing."

"No," he said. "The air is cool, but the water is warm. I am dripping all over your rug, though."

"Do you have anything on under that?"

Devon grinned. "Depends on what you have in mind."

"Take your mind out of the gutter, Taylor. I was talking about drying off."

He laughed and upzipped the wet suit to reveal a bathing suit underneath. His chest hair was damp, a dark golden patch that narrowed before disappearing below his waistband. Brooke had a hard time looking away, his body was too hard, too masculine, too virile to warrant only a passing glance.

Forcing herself to turn, she stopped short of running toward the linen closet. "Here," she said, handing him an oversize bath towel. "Dry off."

"Thanks."

He stepped out of the suit and put it outside on the deck, then toweled down. Brooke stood mesmerized as his hands ran roughshod across his chest, arms and legs. When he threw the towel over his head to dry his hair, she took the opportunity to study him. His legs were long and muscular, and the bathing suit, though boxer style, was short enough and tight enough to give definition to what lay beneath.

She felt her face burn. She'd been too long without a man. And this man, of all available men, was the worst possible choice to change that situation. In her mind, she knew that to be true, but her body and her heart had memories of their own that weren't so easily dismissed. Her pulse quickened and throbbed with a message that seemed to drown out all sound around her. The towel fell from his eyes. As if he heard her siren's call, Devon's blue eyes darkened and locked with hers.

Brooke licked her lips. "Have you eaten...dinner?"

"No," he said, his mouth forming a slow smile.

"Would you like to join me?"

"I'd love to."

"It's only leftover meat loaf," she said as she ushered him into the kitchen.

"Sounds great. I haven't had anything today."

She turned to him as she put the glass dish into the microwave and punched the buttons. "Busy day."

"You, too?" he asked.

"You really shook up the town, Devon."

"Meant to. I needed to get everyone's attention."

"You certainly did that."

He leaned against the doorjamb and crossed one leg over the other. She decided he was too big for her little kitchen. He overpowered the room. He overpowered her. She suddenly needed some space.

"Let's eat in the den. It's cool enough to make a fire, isn't it?"

"Sure," he said, and followed her into the small adjacent room. "Here, let me," he said, taking the flint from her fingers.

As he hunkered down to light the fire, Brooke folded her hands in front of her to prevent her from reaching out and stroking his broad back. This was not good, *definitely* not good. If she was going to continue to deal with him, she was going to have to cover him up.

She excused herself and rummaged through her closet to find an old bathrobe of Andrew's she knew was in there somewhere. Shaking out the old navy velour robe, and holding it in front of her, she realized it would be too small. She sighed. It would have to do. She couldn't bear the thought of sitting next to a half-naked Devon while she ate her dinner.

The fire was catching and sparks flew as she reentered the room.

"What's that?" Devon asked.

"A robe. I thought you might be chilly."

Devon looked at the blazing fire, then back at Brooke. He grinned. "Sure, babe, hand it over."

He slipped his arms through the robe. The sleeves came to a little below his elbows, and it reached to the tops of his knees. He couldn't shut the front, but wrapped the belt around his waist. It covered, as far as Brooke was concerned, several areas that were vital to her peace of mind.

"Better?" he asked as he modeled it for her.

"Much," she said.

The microwave pinged, and he helped her dish out the meat loaf. They carried their plates back inside and sat on the sofa and love seat in front of the fire.

Brooke watched him eat. He seemed so at ease, yet her insides were jumping around like Mexican beans. Fifteen years had passed since she'd last seen him, yet she could still remember everything about him in vivid detail... the look in his eyes just before he kissed her, the feel of his hands massaging her back, the hardness of his body as it strained against hers in the moonlight...

She shook her head. Silly thoughts. Dangerous thoughts.

"How about some coffee?" she asked when they had finished eating.

"Sure. If it's not too much trouble."

"No trouble. It's already made. And I have a great brandy to go with it."

In no time she returned with two brandy snifters and mugs of coffee.

"Mmm," Devon said as he sipped first the coffee, then the brandy. "This is great."

Brooke smiled. She let the warmth of the fire and his approval baste her.

"You mentioned moving your mother back to Lenape Bay. Were you serious?"

"Yep. As soon as the project is finished, I'll send for her," he said without the least hesitation. "I plan to do some work around the house, fixing it up. Besides you and Chuck, no one loved that old place better than my mother."

Brooke felt uncomfortable with his reference to the fact that his mother had cleaned house for her family. He had always been sensitive about it. Was that still the case? She didn't know. That was the trouble. This new, improved Devon was an unknown commodity.

"How is she?" Brooke asked.

"If you're asking if she's over my father's death, I'd have to say yes, she is. She's come a long way in the last few years, especially after I began to make some money and she could quit working." He stared down into the brandy and swirled it around. "I owe her a lot."

"I remember her as being a very quiet, private person. She didn't socialize much."

Devon returned a derisive laugh. "Well, being the mother of the town's hell-raiser didn't exactly get her invited out a lot."

"I'm sorry."

He stared at her over the rim of the brandy glass. "I've often wondered about that over the years."

"About what?"

"About you being sorry."

"It was just an expression, Devon. I wasn't apologizing to you. *I* have nothing to apologize for."

"No, you wouldn't think so, would you?" he asked, more to himself than her.

"Devon—"

"Let's drop it, Brooke. Old news." He swallowed the last of the brandy.

Brooke couldn't believe his audacity. She shook her head, refusing to give him the satisfaction of knowing that she was still bothered by any of the past. As he placed the empty glass on the table, she reached to refill it, and their hands touched. She stared down at her fingers touching his. It took her a moment to realize that Devon had also stopped moving and was staring at her.

"What is it?" she asked.

"You. You've changed. All grown up."

"It had to happen sometime."

He shrugged. "I guess. It's just a little bit of culture shock for me. Coming back to town, seeing everyone again. Everything...everyone's the same...just older."

"You, too," she said.

"Yeah. Me, too." He leaned toward her and took her hand. "It's good to be with you, Brooke. There were a lot of times over the years I wondered what happened to you."

Then why didn't you ever call, or write?

Brooke felt the pang deep inside and pulled her hand away. "That was a long time ago, Devon. You said it yourself yesterday. The past is over."

"You're right. But there is something about you that brings it all back to me, full force. I don't know why that is, but I can't seem to help it."

She looked into depths of blue, and hated herself for wanting to believe him. She didn't, of course. She knew better.

This whole scene was crazy. The two of them, sitting in front of the fire, so cozy, so domestic, so intimate, she couldn't help but feel her antennae go up and stand on end.

"Why are you here, Devon?"

He sat back on the sofa. "I told you. I saw your car from the bay and decided to stop over."

"Spur of the moment."

"Yeah."

"No ulterior motive?"

"None."

Brooke lifted his dirty plate and stacked it on top of hers. She walked past him into the kitchen. Devon followed.

"Why do you think I stopped in?"

"Maybe to get information." She filled the sink and rubbed a soapy sponge against the surface of the plate, then rinsed it.

"About the project? I can get that by making a call to Chuck. He's just dying to tell me all he knows. There were three messages on my machine when I got back in the house this afternoon. I don't need you, babe, not for information."

Brooke threw the sponge into the water and turned to him. "Then what do you need me for, Devon? Why all the interest all of a sudden, after all these years? It's been dead and buried a long time."

His jaw clenched, and she saw the tic in his cheek a split second before he closed in on her.

"Maybe it's not dead, maybe it's only been sleeping." His arms went around her and pulled her up against him as his head descended. "Let's find out."

His mouth was hot, and it took hers in a searing kiss that allowed no dissent. Devon angled his head for better access as he lifted her into him. His hand entwined in her hair to massage her scalp as he held her in place.

This was no gentle touching of one set of lips to another. It was more like a brushfire gone out of control into a swirling inferno. From the moment his mouth touched hers, Brooke knew she was gone, lost in a world of forgotten sensation, a dangerous, erotic world that for too long had only existed in her imagination.

Brooke clung to his shoulder with one hand, at first to stave him off, but when his tongue touched hers, his heat penetrated deep inside, and she couldn't stop her fingers from clutching him closer to her.

The tastes of coffee, brandy and sea intermingled. She felt rather than heard the soft moan escape from the back of her throat and lose itself in him. She touched his chest with her other hand, ran her fingers though the soft golden curls, and felt herself go limp in his arms.

She had been a married woman, had tasted passion in the arms of a man, but this...this was something else again, something beyond her experience, something pure, wild, right, wrong, and so delicious she could hardly stand another moment of it, yet she never wanted it to end.

Her legs gave way, and Devon pushed his hips into her, wedging her between his body and the kitchen counter. She could feel his need, and instinctively she responded to it with her own sweet pressure. That was all the invitation Devon needed. He moved his hands down her sides to her bottom and lifted her against him as his mouth and tongue continued to devour hers. Raw desire snaked through her, and she gave herself up to it.

She had no idea how long it lasted. Time gave way to sensation and had no meaning. It was Devon who pulled back, pushed away. He was breathing heavily, his eyes so bright they blazed like beacons in the night. Brooke grabbed hold of the counter for support. She stared back at him, too dazed to speak, too numb to feel.

"I think that answers the question, don't you?"

He slipped out of the robe, laid it across a chair, and headed for the patio door. Brooke followed him.

"Where are you going?" she asked, finally finding her voice.

"Back."

"You can't ride that Jet Ski in the dark. It's too dangerous out there."

He pulled the door open and stepped outside, picking up his wet suit on the way. When he turned back to her, he had that half-smirk on his face. "Not as dangerous as in here, babe. Not by half."

Four

Brooke arrived at her office early to get a head start on work she had been neglecting. With her assistant, Joan, out sick, she knew she'd have her hands full. She took a sip of hot coffee from her I'm The Boss mug and settled in for a full morning. She made fast work of sorting through the mail, and checking through the messages piled up by her phone.

For all appearances, it was business as usual. The day was bright, sunny and still unseasonably warm. Yet, to Brooke, nothing seemed the same since Devon had reappeared in her life. The very air around town was charged, filling her with renewed energy.

As much as she struggled against it, the past still haunted her. Devon's unexpected visit two nights ago had opened a floodgate of memories that, try as she might, she couldn't wish away.

Brooke fiddled with the papers and pens on her desk, moving them from the right to the left and back again before realizing what she was doing. She knew she needed to review quotes on the road repair work project, but as she stared down at the letter in front of her, the words blurred.

She was fidgety, restless. She was angry, too, with herself for her reaction to Devon, for letting him get the upper hand, for letting him get close to her...for letting him kiss her.

Stop it!

But that was the problem. She couldn't *stop* it. Thoughts of him were creeping into her mind all the time. It was making her nervous. It was making her scared.

Years ago, when he'd left her, she'd fantasized about how she would react if they should ever meet again. She would be aloof, cool, so unbothered by his presence, she would barely acknowledge it, except with perhaps an I-don't-care smile and a nod. Well, she'd grown up, and was adult enough to realize that she would have to communicate with the man.

Communicate meant talk, not kiss.

She could have pushed him away, could have told him off in no uncertain terms. No, she had to respond to him, welcome him as if she was dying of thirst, and he was an oasis. Her stomach clenched at the memory of his mouth on hers. The kiss *was* something else. Something desperate, sultry, and hot as a summer night. Every buried sensation had risen to the surface on a tidal wave of emotion.

And all with just one kiss.

Swiveling in her chair, Brooke stared out her second-floor window. People were coming and going in and out of the various shops that lined the main drag. She heard the hammering below at the same time she noticed the pickup truck parked in front of her building.

"What in the world . . . ?"

Brooke left her office and made her way toward the reception area, passing Joan's vacant desk. The building was a duplex, offering high ceilings and lots of skylights. She shared the second floor with the tax assessor's office, but the space below had been empty for the past few months. She descended the spiral staircase to the first-floor landing, following the sound to the office door.

With a slight shove of her hand, the door swung open to reveal a large room furnished with only one metal desk. Devon was on a stepladder at the far corner of the room, his back to her. The noise obliterated her entry. Brooke stepped inside and shut the door behind her.

He was dressed casually in a T-shirt and jeans, both a bit too snug. His body was solid, tight, and his muscles flexed as he hammered. He must work out, she thought, then wondered why, with all the things she had to say to him, that thought would be the first to jump into her head.

At that moment he stopped hammering and climbed down the ladder. Turning, he noticed her immediately.

"Hello, Brooke."

"Devon."

For the longest moment they stood, a room and a past separating them. She hadn't seen him since the night he'd kissed her and had to fight the desire to flee. He held her gaze with eyes completely devoid of any of the discomfort she felt. She envied him that. Part of her wanted to dig a hole in the floor and crawl into it. The other part of her wanted him to kiss her again.

She looked away, shifted her weight, and adjusted her navy blazer to cover her awkwardness.

"What's up?" he asked as he lifted a shelf from the floor.

Devon climbed back up the ladder and carefully fitted the shelf into the brackets on the wall. Brooke felt more comfortable with his back to her, and she moved into the center of the room. Unwittingly, her gaze traveled from his legs up his strong thighs and tight buttocks to the wide span of his shoulders.

"Brooke?"

"Hmm?"

"What can I do for you?" Devon said as he turned to her.

She looked up at his face. His eyes were clear, bright, well-rested and so wide opened she felt as if she could fall into them.

"What are you doing?" she asked.

"I'm putting up shelves."

"I can see that. Why here?"

"I've rented the place. I need an office in town." He climbed down the ladder and lifted the second shelf.

"And y_____ _____ _____ _____ _____?"

Devo_____

"I do_____

"Then_____

availab_____

turned_____

Br_____

He looked at her over his shoulder and graced her with his half smile. "So we finally get to the point."

"And that is . . . ?"

Devon climbed down and walked toward her. "Your problem. *Me*. Being here. Being back in town. Right?"

"Right."

"Why is that, Brooke?"

"You know why," she answered.

He shook his head. "No, I don't. Tell me."

"I don't trust you, Devon. Nor do I believe you when you say you're here to stay. Whatever it is you're doing, I don't want you doing it here. You're up to something. I can feel it."

"Telephone?"

Both Devon and Brooke turned to the serviceman standing in the doorway.

Devon pointed to the metal desk. "Over there will be fine."

The two held each other's gaze in defiant silence as the serviceman went about his business. Devon broke eye contact first. Hand on hip, he blew out an annoyed breath and looked past her to the front window, pre-tending to study

attitude
uth, but
te pain in
t she'd

es as

they all would respond like puppets. It seemed simple, and right up until two nights ago it had been.

Then he'd kissed her.

That had been his first mistake. He had forgotten how he'd always reacted to her, forgotten how her hazel eyes would mist over whenever he came too near. He'd forgotten how that wistful, come-hither look could turn him from stony ice to sizzling steam.

Fifteen years was a damned long time. He had forgotten too much.

Like her softness, like how she felt in his arms, like how she melted against him . . . like how she tasted. His mouth watered, and he shuffled from one foot to the other to alleviate the rising pressure in his tight jeans.

This had to stop. *He* had to stop it. It wasn't what he wanted, and definitely not what he needed. She was dangerous, very dangerous, and that thought alone sent his blood rushing through his veins at an alarming speed. He had to take control of the situation, and fast. There was only one way to deal with an adversary, and that was to attack.

When he returned his attention to her, his eyes were narrow, intense. "Did you ever stop to think that what you're feeling has nothing to do with me, but with yourself?"

"Don't be ridiculous."

"Think about it, Brooke. You're the only one in town who's fighting this project, fighting me. Why is that?"

Brooke clenched her teeth. "I don't know, Devon. You seem to know it all. Why don't you tell me?"

"One line or two?" the serviceman called.

"Two," Devon answered.

He grabbed hold of Brooke's elbow and walked her to the door. "Now isn't a good time to discuss this. Why don't you come to the house tonight? I owe you a dinner. We can talk. You can ask me any questions you want, and I'll promise to answer them."

"I don't want to have dinner with you."

"What are you afraid of?"

"Fear has nothing to do with it. It's trust we're talking about," she said.

"Ah, yes. Trust. You keep using that word. Interesting coming from your lips," he said.

"What, pray tell, is that supposed to mean, Devon?"

"Come tonight and find out."

"I don't—"

"You want another outlet on the other side?" the serviceman called again.

"Hold on a second," Devon answered the man. "I'll be right with you." He opened the door for Brooke and ushered her out into the hallway.

"Tonight. Seven o'clock." He began to shut the door, then peeked around it. "Oh. And bring the wine."

Brooke stared at the blank door, dumbstruck. He did it again, just took over and called all the shots. No, she *allowed* him to do it again.

It was her own fault. Her first mistake had been to invite him into her home when he showed up at her back door. What she should have done was ask him to state his business while standing on the porch, then bid him good-night. But no, good old Brooke had to invite him inside, ask him to share her dinner *and* a brandy. She even lit a fire.

The entire setting must have seemed like an open invitation to him. Did he think she was coming on to him? Even the thought of him *thinking* that she wanted him was enough to send her stomach into an Olympic somersault.

Brooke marched back up to her office. As she entered, the hammering started again, and the image of his muscles flexing with the exertion zapped into her head. She groaned. She couldn't stay here, not another moment. Opening the bottom drawer of her desk, she pulled out her handbag and headed down the stairs, into the street and straight to Pattersen Central Bank.

Brooke nodded toward the guard as she made her way toward her brother's office. Her heels click-clacked on the marble floor, reinforcing her decision to act rather than *re*act. If she wanted her life back, she most definitely had to do something about Devon Taylor.

She had to get rid of him.

Chuck was sitting behind his desk, the phone cradled between his shoulder and ear. As he answered the person on the other end, he motioned to Brooke to come in and sit down. She did, but when it became obvious that her brother was in no hurry to end his conversation, she dropped her bag beside the chair and paced until he hung up.

"Hiya, Brooke. Come about the barbecue?"

"What barbecue?" she asked.

"The one Lotty and I are planning. Didn't she call you?"

"No, she didn't. What are we celebrating?"

"It's in honor of Devon Taylor and the Maiden Point project. Kind of a kickoff party, you know?" Chuck said.

"What *is* going on with Devon's Maiden Point project?" she asked.

Chuck grinned. "Great, isn't it? We're all very excited. The papers are ready to be signed."

"I can't believe you're taking him seriously, let alone approving loans and giving him a party," Brooke said as she continued to pace. "You, of all people."

"Sit down, Brooke," Chuck said. "You're making me nervous."

Brooke stopped. "You should be nervous." She took a seat across from him. "This project can literally break the bank."

"Don't you think I know that? I've checked into his prospectus personally, and all my contacts are coming back positive. This could be the biggest deal Pattersen Central Bank ever put together. Bigger than anything Daddy ever did."

Brooke bit her lip. Chuck was forever comparing himself to Chaz, and though she knew he needed her reassurance, she couldn't bring herself to give it. Not in this instance.

"I just don't see you doing business with Devon Taylor. Not after all that's happened between you," Brooke said, getting to what she considered the heart of the subject.

"That was a long time ago. Kid stuff. We're talking money now, real money, Brooke, and I'm not going to let any past nonsense about Devon stop me from getting a piece of this."

"You hate him, Chuck."

"I *hated* him. I don't anymore."

"Why? Because now he has money?"

"No, because he's changed."

Brooke snorted.

"If you don't believe he's changed, then why did you invite him to your cottage the other night?" Chuck asked.

"I didn't... How did you kno

Chuck shrugged. "I stopped by the old house this morning. Devon told me."

Great, Brooke thought, just great. Devon and Chuck sitting around my old kitchen table talking about old times . . . how nauseatingly cozy!

"Did you also know he rented the space in my building?" she asked.

"Sure I knew. I'm the one who told him it was available."

Brooke stared at her brother incredulously. She took a deep breath and shook her head. "This is so bizarre, I can't stand it."

"For heaven's sake, Brooke, it's been fifteen years. Don't tell me you're still carrying a torch for the guy after all this time."

"Don't be absurd," Brooke said. "I have less than no interest in the man."

"Then what is it?" Chuck asked.

"I just seem to have a better memory than you. In case you've forgotten, let me remind you. He had more than a passing dislike for this town, and he never hid his feelings about you, or Daddy, *or* this bank!" Brooke said as she pointed to the front window that had been replaced fifteen years ago.

"So? He apologized to me about that night."

"He apologized *to you!*" she exploded. "And that makes it all right?"

Chuck smiled. "So that's it."

"That's *what?*" She was really getting angry.

"You're bothered because Devon didn't apologize to you for taking off. If that's all it is, then let me explain what happened—"

Brooke held up her hand and cut him off. Having this conversation with her brother was about as useless as talking to the bank's infamous front window.

"Please, Chuck, don't bother. I think I can take care of Devon Taylor all by myself." She stood. "It's obvious that now is not a good time to go into this. You've got too many stars in your eyes. Let's talk again when you've finished your investigation into this consortium of his. Then, maybe we'll have something substantial to work with."

Chuck stood. "Suit yourself. But I think you're all wrong about him. He's changed. He really has."

Brooke slipped her bag over her shoulder as she opened the office door. "How has he changed, Chuck? Can you tell me?"

"Oh, I don't know exactly. Let me think." He bit his lower lip for a moment, then pointed his index finger at her. "He's more in control now. That's what it is. Devon never could control himself very well. It's what made him so dangerous and unpredictable."

Brooke hung on to the door for a long moment, staring back at her brother. For all his shallowness, every once in a while Chuck would hit the nail on the head. He was right. Devon *was* more in control now.

The Devon of long ago would have never stopped with just one kiss.

Without a wave good-bye, she walked out of the bank into the sunshine. While Chuck's remark was meant to reassure her, it did quite the contrary.

Devon in control. She felt a chill run down her back. Now, *that* was a scary thought.

Brooke began walking slowly back to her office, then changed her mind. Seeing Devon again would only serve to aggravate her more. She headed to the parking lot to get her car. A quick stop over at the municipal center would keep her busy enough to forget all about what happened this morning…as well as stop her from thinking about tonight.

As she passed Ye Olde Spirits Shoppe, an idea hit her. Chuck was right, bless his little heart. This *was* all about control, wasn't it? Who has it, who needs it, and why? If that was the case, then she'd been handling Devon all wrong. She'd been letting him have his way with her— so to speak—and it was time to call a immediate halt to that course of action.

The fact remained that Devon Taylor had something she wanted: the truth. The question was: what did she have that Devon wanted? The only thing Devon had ever wanted from her was her body. Could she handle that? Could she tempt him to tell the truth, play Mata Hari and use herself for bait, without hurting herself in the end?

Years ago she would have had to say no to that question. But today was different. She was different. All grown up, and not a naive teenage girl anymore. And getting the truth out of him was important to her, to the bank and to the town. He'd trusted her once, a long time ago, and he could trust her again—and maybe, just maybe she'd find out what he was really up to before it was too late.

Brooke felt a surge of confidence. She could handle him, perhaps better than anyone else in town, because when all was said and done, no one knew him better than she. She couldn't depend on anyone else to get rid of him. It was fate, justice. She had to do it herself. With conviction oozing out of every pore, Brooke entered the liquor store.

First things first. She needed a bottle of wine.

Five

Devon admired the roast, ladling juice from the bottom of the pan over the meat. The aroma made his stomach growl, and he checked the thermometer to see that it was already half done. Before shutting the oven door, he stuck a fork into the baking potatoes and decided that his timing was perfect. Everything would be ready at once.

He wiped his brow with the back of his hand, and poured himself a glass of Burgundy. He'd become quite the cook during his time living alone, at first due to necessity, then as the years went by, because he enjoyed it. He was no gourmet, but could easily find his way around a kitchen.

It had become a point of pride with him. Whenever he'd meet a new woman, inevitably she'd ask to come over and cook for him. It pleased him to be able to turn the tables. He supposed it had to do with his contrary nature. Never do what people expect you to do; always keep them guessing.

It worked before; it was working now. Brooke was thoroughly confused, and that was just how he wanted her to be. She didn't believe him, but she wanted to, and that fact alone would see him through to his end.

There was a time when it would have bothered him to do something this underhanded to her, but she'd been a good teacher. She taught him that words were easy to come by; actions were something else.

Yet Devon was nothing if not honest with himself. *He* was his biggest problem with Brooke. He was still very attracted to her. His body had come to life when he'd kissed her, and had awakened powerful, old feelings. His reasonable, sane mind told him it would be best if he didn't spend time alone with her. After that kiss, he had lectured himself relentlessly on the wisdom of such action. So, of course, he had done the exact opposite and invited her over for dinner tonight.

The thought of Brooke as an invited guest in her former home was too sweet to pass up. He wanted to watch her in these rooms, roaming around, touching the furniture, reminiscing. During the first year or two after he'd left, he'd dreamt about this house and a night such as this. Having only his mother's occasional comment to go on, he would fantasize about how each room looked. He'd pictured himself sitting in front of the fireplace, slippered feet resting on an antique ottoman, brandy snifter in hand, with Brooke dressed in a black-and-white maid's outfit serving him.

Adolescent thoughts, he mused, but very powerful nevertheless. While he no longer wished to see her serve him, he still harbored the desire to entertain her in this house—now *his* house. Would it cause her pain? He didn't know. Brooke and the rest of the Pattersens always seemed impervious to such common feelings as pain. They seemed to breeze through life, capable of very few deep emotions, save perhaps hate.

Yes, they knew how to hate very well.

Some might think it strange that he wished to live in the house of his old enemy, but Devon had always had a fascination for this place, ever since he was small. He remembered the first time his father drove him past it in his pickup when he was seven or so. At the time, Jack and Chaz were still doing business together, and Jack had to drop off some papers early one Saturday morning.

Devon had been told to sit in the truck, and for all his hyper energy, he had obeyed. He'd spent the time studying the pink-and-gray turrets and imagining himself climbing up the side to reach the top balcony. More than anything, he'd wanted to go inside and see what the rooms upstairs looked like, how they were shaped, and how the bay would look from such a high vantage point.

Now he knew. He'd taken over the master bedroom suite overlooking the bay. It had been Chaz's old room, and as he lay in the oversize four-poster upstairs each night, he experienced a sense of homecoming that he had never felt before in his life. He was forming an attachment to the old place. That was not on his agenda . . . any more than getting involved with Brooke was.

Inviting her to dinner had a twofold purpose. First, of course, to ease her mind about the project, but there was no doubt that the second reason was just as important to him as the first. He had a serious hankering for the woman; time hadn't changed that. Once it would have been as deadly to him as a diabetic craving a chocolate-covered cherry. But no more. This wasn't love he was talking about. Nothing she could say or do could reignite that fire. It was the one thing of which he was absolutely sure.

His heart was safe.

The doorbell rang, and a jolt of pure pleasure shot through his veins. He took a final sip before placing his wineglass on the counter. He smiled. The idea of Brooke waiting for *him* to allow *her* entrance to her old home was a moment worth savoring.

With a quick glance to the heavens, he pulled at the heavy oak door. *Are you watching, Chaz?*

But what Devon saw quickly dispelled any thoughts of revenge.

"Hello, Devon."

Brooke stood before him dressed in the tightest, skimpiest, royal blue knit dress he'd ever seen. Every curve on her body was accentuated. The dress was long-sleeved, low-cut, and so short, it stopped somewhere midthigh. Ignoring his bewildered expression, Brooke passed slowly in front of him, presenting him with a geometric cutout that displayed a good portion of her back.

"Did they run out of fabric?" he asked.

Brooke looked down at herself with wide-eyed innocence. "Don't you like it?"

He shut the door. "I like it fine."

"Your wine," Brooke said as she held the bottle out to him.

Devon was in shock. He attempted to hide it by pretending to study the expensive French label. It was a futile act of self-preservation. His eyes kept returning to the woman before him. Brooke stared back at him, almost defiantly challenging him to find something wrong with her. He couldn't. She was perfect. Her chestnut hair was windblown full and beckoned him to run his fingers through it. Her makeup was artistically applied, right down to a glossy, pouting, rosebud mouth, and that dress . . . it was close enough to indecent to set his libido on "simmer."

Devon pulled his gaze away from her obviously braless cleavage and returned his attention to the safety of the wine bottle.

"Good year," he said.

"Surprised?"

"Not really. The Pattersens always surrounded themselves with the best of everything. I've come to enjoy that." He indicated the room in which they were standing with a wave of his hand . . . but his eyes never left her.

Brooke resisted the temptation to cross her arms over her chest. He was staring; that was good. Judging from his reaction, the dress was more than worth the week's salary she'd invested in it.

As nonchalantly as possible, she surveyed her old family living room that her father had always referred to as the "parlor." Devon had obviously had a service in to spruce the place up. It was neat, cleaned and polished. The furniture was placed differently, but still had the comfortable look she loved. A pang of longing pierced her heart, but she took a deep breath and sent it on its way. There was no room for nostalgia. She had a job to do.

"The room looks wonderful. It's good to see it in use again," she said.

He ushered her to the sitting area and poured her a glass of Burgundy from a carafe on the coffee table.

"It's usable, but the house needs an awful lot of work. I've got some ideas on renovation. When I get them down on paper, I'd like you to look them over, if you would." He tried, unsuccessfully, to keep his gaze at eye level.

"So, you really are planning to stay?" she asked as she sat on the sofa and crossed her legs.

The skirt was much too short, and that was a fact. Devon felt as if his head was on one planet, his body on another. He couldn't stop his gaze from roaming from one strategic spot on her body to the next.

He cleared his throat. "I thought I'd made that clear. I'd like to restore it to its original beauty. You'd be the best one to advise me on that, don't you think?"

"I suppose." Brooke watched his eyes lock onto the juncture of her crossed legs. She had to consciously refrain from tugging at the hem of her skirt.

"Unless you'd find it too difficult . . . having me living in your family home and all," Devon said.

Brooke sipped the wine, carefully studying him. "The only thing I find difficult, Devon, is believing you."

He sat next to her. He had to. There was no choice. "What can I say to prove I'm sincere?" he asked softly.

He was close, too close. Heat radiated from his body, his scent was clean, masculine. Brooke stared into crystal-blue eyes and almost forgot the question.

She lowered her gaze. "The truth, Devon. Tell me the truth."

He lifted her chin. Giving in to impulse, he threaded his fingers into her hair and held her steady. Luminous hazel eyes stared into his, and Devon felt his stomach drop. He wanted to kiss her. No, not just kiss her. Devour her.

"The truth? The truth is, Brooke, that I want to—"

The buzzer sounded; the roast was done. Devon dropped his hands. "Dinner," he said, almost apologetically, and headed into the kitchen.

Brooke smiled cordially as he left the room, then quickly gulped down the remainder of the wine. She rose, and smoothed the sides of the dress over her hips and thighs. She was nervous. Her skin glowed with a fine sheen of perspiration, yet her hands were ice cold. She spread them against her flushed cheeks to cool her fevered skin.

Playing the seductress was hard work, she discovered, and she wasn't at all sure that she was cut out for it. She was too much the amateur, and he, no doubt, had experience galore. Be that as it may, she seemed to be succeeding. He hadn't been able to take his eyes from her, and she hoped that before the night was over, she'd be well on her way to finding out what Devon was really about.

With a swallow and a breath, she headed for the kitchen, striking a pose as she leaned a hip against the doorway.

Devon was carving the small roast. He almost sliced his hand as he glanced her way. Those legs encased in black hose and high heels seemed to go on forever, conjuring up all sorts of images.

"Can I help?" she asked.

"Sure," he said, forcing his attention back to his task. "Salad's in the fridge. Give it a toss and set it on the dining room table."

Languidly, Brooke pushed herself off the door frame and ambled over to the refrigerator. After following his directions, she carried the silver bowl into the dining room and placed it in the center of the table.

Devon stopped carving. He gaped as she lifted one leg slightly and bent over just far enough to give him an unrestricted view of her tight, round derriere.

She turned quickly and caught him. "Anything else?" she asked.

And then he caught the smile.

It was a thoroughly satisfied, absolutely female smile. Devon stared at her for the longest moment as the realization hit him. She was enticing him. On purpose. He should have guessed immediately. The dress, the makeup, the sultry moves, were so out of character for Brooke, his antennae should have picked up the warning signs as soon as he'd opened the door.

Why? he wondered. What was her game? He returned the smile, a slow half-grin that should have told her he was on to her. Her reason didn't matter, not in the least. It was a game he knew well.

And two could play it.

"Sit, and make yourself comfortable."

As she took the seat to the right of the head of the table, Brooke thought she heard him laugh. She leaned forward and peeked into the kitchen from her seat to check him out just as he entered the room carrying a steaming platter of meat and potatoes.

"Hungry?" he asked as he filled her plate.

"Starved," she answered.

He took the seat across from her, and their eyes met. "Me, too."

The food was steamy hot and cooked to perfection. Brooke admitted to him that his cooking skills were more than adequate. The meal was surprisingly pleasant, and she found herself thoroughly enjoying it as well as the company. She helped him serve dessert and coffee, but demurred when he reached across to refill her brandy glass.

"No more for me," she said, more than mellow already. "You promised to answer my questions about the project."

"Ask away," he said as he swirled the contents of his brandy glass.

"Let's start with the consortium. Who are these people, Devon?"

He sat forward and rested his elbows on the table. "They are friends of mine, Brooke. People with whom I've had successful business dealings over the past ten or so years."

"And they readily invest in your projects, sight unseen?" she asked.

"Yes."

"I don't understand, Devon. Maiden Point will cost a lot of money."

"And the consortium will make a lot of money. I've done this before, Brooke. *They* trust me."

"Unlike me," she said.

"Unlike you."

His gaze locked with hers for a long moment. Then he did the strangest thing. He laughed. Brooke's eyebrows crinkled.

"You're much too serious, Brooke. You always were. Here," he said as he picked up a chocolate-covered strawberry, "Indulge a little. Open up."

"This is serious, Devon."

He dangled the strawberry in front of her lips. "Open."

"No."

"It's sweet."

"I don't want it."

"Just a bite."

"Dev—"

He pushed the fruit into her mouth, and she had no choice except to bite into it. He was right; it was sweet. And juicy. She took a second bite, and grazed the pad of his thumb with her teeth.

Devon's eyes darkened with the contact. He dropped the stem onto the dish, then rubbed his thumb against her lower lip before pulling away. Brooke felt her insides tremble in confusion at the sensations his touch aroused. Her hand shook as she lifted the napkin to her lips.

This time when he attempted to refill her brandy glass, she let him. She needed something to steady her nerves.

Devon clinked his glass to hers. "To Lenape Bay and Maiden Point."

Hesitantly she brought the glass to her lips. "To Lenape Bay," she said, not quite ready to toast the rest.

As she took a sip of brandy, she shut her eyes, welcoming its warmth. For all her bravado, she was tense, and rolled her head to the left, then the right, trying to work out the kinks.

"Tired?" Devon asked.

"A little," she said. "It's been a long day." She rubbed the nape of her neck with her hand.

Devon rose and walked behind her chair. "Let me," he said.

Before she could protest, Devon began massaging the back of her neck. His hands were large, their span reaching from shoulder to shoulder. His touch was dry and firm as he worked magic with her tight muscles. Brooke couldn't help but groan at the mixture of pleasure and pain.

"Feel good?"

"Mmm."

"Let's get this out of the way."

Devon unbuttoned the top of her dress to give him better access. Startled, Brooke reached up to her chest to hold the fabric in place as it fell forward.

"Devon—"

"Shh," he said. "Relax."

His hands were all over her, from her hairline down the length of her spine, across her shoulder blades. His fingers dug into her muscles . . . warm, strong, vibrant. She knew she shouldn't allow him to touch her like this, but she was mellow from the wine and brandy. Besides, the sensations were so luxurious, so deliciously decadent, she couldn't conjure up enough indignation to tell him to stop.

Devon leaned over her as he pressed his fingers into her flesh. His breath fanned the top of her head. He inhaled her scent, the warm, woman smell of her body, and his own body stirred in response. Shutting his eyes, he moved his hands over her back, receiving as much pleasure as he was giving. More. His hands roamed up her shoulders and around to her collarbone. Her skin was so soft, so smooth, he was afraid he'd mark her, so he lightened the pressure until his fingers were merely skimming the surface.

Devon leaned forward and looked down at her. Her head was bent, eyes closed, and she was breathing deeply, her chest heaving ever so slightly as his hands became bolder. He watched as her nipples tightened, puckering to pebbles under the thin, knit fabric. Unable and unwilling to stop himself, Devon reached inside the front of her dress and cupped her full breasts.

"Devon!"

"Just let me touch you," he said softly as he continued to gently massage her. "God, you feel so good...so soft... I've never forgotten how soft your skin is. All those years ago, and I still remember your softness."

Devon nuzzled her neck, and Brooke gave up the fight. She was dizzy from the heat of his mouth and the feel of his hands on her sensitive breasts. His hot breath seared her skin as his hands continued to set her on fire. A slow, liquid pool of want burst inside her, and she went limp, giving herself to him and whatever he wanted to do with her.

Devon was wild. He was caught in a web of his own making. A voice of reason somewhere deep inside told him to save himself, to stop touching her, but it seemed as if his hands had a mind of their own. Fascinated, he watched himself caress her, his hands hidden beneath the fabric of her dress. He resisted the urge to pull the dress away and see her. Instead he tempted himself further as he slowly drew circles around her already taut nipples. Then he cupped her breasts, one in each hand, and flicked his thumbs across the tiny, pouting orbs.

She whimpered, and he felt himself grow hard and swell. He kissed her neck, his mouth open and wet against her heated skin. She was so soft, as silky smooth as melting French vanilla ice cream. More than anything, he wanted to taste each tempting peak.

Somewhere in the deep recesses of her mind, Brooke dimly recalled why she'd come tonight. Something about the town, the bank, the truth. But it all seemed vague and unimportant now. The only thing that mattered was Devon. His mouth, his hands, and the way he was touching her. She wanted to turn in his arms, kiss him, take him inside of her and keep him there... forever.

The word froze her.

With Devon, there was no such thing as forever.

Devon noticed the change immediately, as her entire body tightened. "What is it?" he asked.

"I have to leave," she said, and pushed herself away from him and the table.

"Brooke—"

"No, Devon, really. It's late. It was a lovely dinner, but I have to go."

Head down, too embarrassed to look at him, Brooke reached around and rebuttoned the back of her dress. When she did turn, he was standing a few feet away, his eyes bright, intense. He had both hands in his pants' pockets . . . a ploy that hid nothing. She forced her gaze to move up to his face, knowing full well that her own was flushed.

"I won't apologize," he said.

"I'm not asking you to. It was as much my fault as yours."

"Maybe more. You were looking for something tonight, Brooke. I hope you found it."

She grabbed her bag and headed for the door. "What I wanted was the truth, Devon. The truth about your intentions."

"I told you, babe." He held the door open for her. "What you see is what you get. I'm serious about this project. I'm here to stay."

"I wish I could believe that," she answered as she stepped through the doorway.

Devon grabbed hold of her wrist, brought her hand to his mouth. With eyes never leaving hers, he kissed the center of her palm, a long, openmouthed kiss that ended with the tiniest flicks of his tongue.

"Believe it."

The sound Brooke made was one more of pain than pleasure. It shot through him like an arrow to the heart—that same heart he had thought invincible.

He watched her leave, and for the briefest instant, Devon almost wished he could believe it himself.

Six

Brooke's convertible whizzed down the dirt road leading to the entrance to Maiden Point. She stopped when she saw the sign announcing the renovation project. The new sign was eye-catching with bright colors and attractive lettering, and it deserved a second look.

Just like the project.

Just like the man behind it.

She pressed down on the accelerator and headed for the model apartment in the main building. As she pulled into the parking lot, she noticed that Devon's forest-green Jaguar was not in its usual space near the entrance.

She'd been sent to "fetch" him. Chuck's party was well under way, sans the guest of honor. When they'd called his office, the machine had picked up and advised that he was at the construction site. It was obvious that Devon had forgotten all about it. Since there was no phone at Maiden Point, Chuck suggested—in front of everyone—that Brooke ride out to get Devon. Her protests sounded feeble even to her own ears, so here she was, feeling both foolish and ambivalent.

For it was evident that Devon had been avoiding her since that dinner at his house. She'd see him come into the office or go out, but other than a brief hello and some stilted small talk, he made it his business never to dawdle or make eye contact.

At first she was more than happy with the arrangement. She told herself she didn't want to be with him any more than he wanted to be with her. He made her uncomfortable, aware of too many things, too many feelings ... and after that little episode in his dining room, she acknowledged that it definitely was not safe to be alone with him.

But as the weeks passed, her suspicious nature reared its ugly head once again. She began to wonder why he was being so evasive. What was he hiding? What did he do in that office all day long? Whenever she peeked in, he was on the telephone. Whom was he calling?

She still didn't trust him, no matter how charmingly he crossed his heart or swore he was here to stay, but her misgivings were brushed aside by everyone else. She sounded like a spoilsport instead of the voice of reason. Some of the town council people were cutting short their meetings with her rather than get involved in a discussion on the dubious merits of the Maiden Point project.

Brooke was beginning to feel alienated in her own town. She had always felt as if she belonged here more than anywhere else in the world. In the short time he'd been back, Devon Taylor had changed all that. He had turned her world—and her head—upside-down.

Brooke left the construction site without going inside. Logic told her he must have left, and was probably home by now. Common sense told her to go back to the party and tell Chuck to do his own dirty work, but instead she headed in the direction of the old Victorian.

The front door was open when she arrived, and she stepped over the threshold after her knock went unheeded. She called out for Devon, but no one answered. The foyer was cool as a cross breeze blew in off the bay. Dressed in a watermelon-red, polka dot, sleeveless sundress, Brooke had left her jacket in the car. She wrapped her arms around herself as she searched through the downstairs rooms for Devon.

The kitchen was a mess, with a half-eaten ham sandwich on the table. She dropped her car keys on the counter and peered out back. Devon was at the far end of the dock, on his knees, stripped to the waist, hammering new strips of wood into the crumbling decking. Brooke raised a hand to shield her eyes from the glare of the sun. She grabbed onto the railing to assist herself as she gingerly walked over the cracks in her high-heeled sandals.

The closer she got, the better he looked. Suntanned, his golden body glistened with sweat. Muscles straining, tightening and releasing as he efficiently fused each new piece of wood to the old. Brooke stopped and stood perfectly still, taking this rare opportunity to have her fill of him. She watched the sure, almost graceful motions of his hands as he worked, and remembered only too well how they felt as they moved across her skin.

She shivered from the inside out. He was a magnificent specimen of man, she acknowledged, and no matter what he said, or did, nothing could change her very feminine reaction to that fact.

Before she could speak, Devon threw a few pieces of wood over the deck and jumped down after them. She peered over the side to see him, but he seemed to have disappeared. The breeze lifted her skirt in the air. Trapping it in her hands, Brooke held it down as she leaned against the railing. It was another beautiful day, clear, with just a hint of autumn. Indian Summer at its finest, she thought, and breathed deeply of the clean, salt air.

She turned and searched for him along the expanse of sand as it stretched along the bay. She clutched the railing in a carefree movement as the breeze caught her again.

That's how Devon first saw her as he climbed up onto the deck from behind. She was swaying in the wind, her hair in disarray, her dress billowing. The sun was beginning to graze the horizon, and her lone figure stood out in stark contrast to the vast expanse of cloudless sky.

Devon tilted his head as he seriously studied her. She looked ripe, luscious, as tasty as the watermelon-red and white print of her dress. He liked her best this way when he could unknowingly observe her. He didn't have to pretend then that he felt nothing for her, that she meant nothing to him. He could do that so well when she stared at him with her best, disapproving Pattersen look, but at times like this, he could let his imagination run free and remember when she had looked at him quite differently. Her dreamy, hazel eyes had spoken to him of private things—things that he had buried too deep to be easily resurrected. Too bad today's message wasn't nearly as eloquent as the memory of those eyes.

He moved silently toward her.

Too bad.

Brooke never sensed his presence. Suddenly he was behind her, and she felt a pressure against her back as his hands covered hers on the railing, effectively trapping her. She froze, yet she felt no fear. Shutting her eyes tightly, she willed herself to be still, to let him lead the way, knowing full well that when he did, she would be right there for him. For him to... what?

"This setting reminds me of you, did you know that?" She felt his warm breath in her hair. "For years, I couldn't enjoy the shore at all because of all the memories it brought back."

"Devon—"

"Don't say a word."

The logical side of his mind told him to pull away. He didn't want anything to do with her. He didn't want to *want* her at all, in any way. But the fact was that he did want her. He told himself it was only a physical response to a memory, but knowing it and disregarding it were two different things. The more he saw her, the more he wanted her. And each day brought a new test to his will.

He should back off, start a conversation of small talk and begin the charade again, but he couldn't exert enough energy to pick up the fight where it left off. And it was a fight. With every fiber of his being, he fought the irrational urge to stop this civilized farce and make her his. His fingers entwined with hers, more from a need to keep his hands in place than to hold her still.

He had felt physical desire many times in his life, but this was magnified a thousand times over because of who she was and what he had felt for her then...of what he felt for her now. He tightened his grip on her hands and shut his eyes, resting his chin on the top of her head as he fought for control. It was no use. Her scent drifted over him, and he felt himself swell in response.

It was so crazy, so insane, so dangerous to want her, but the want was there, and it was as real and as vital as the steady beat of his heart. More than anything, he wanted to touch each soft curve of her body, to caress her, absorb her into him. She made him feel safe when all he'd ever felt was adrift. She made him feel strong inside, not out where he already knew his own worth. But best—or worst—of all, she made him *feel*.

Devon took a deep breath and gave in to temptation. He pulled her against him, fitting her round buttocks against him in a way to cushion his hard arousal. Outwardly still, but inwardly wild, he pulsed with the need to make love with her. Right here, right now, on the deck, with the wind blowing through her hair and the sun tucking itself into the sea for the night.

Brooke felt every hard inch of him through the thin material of her dress, and her insides churned. The breeze shifted and cooled, wrapping the material of her full skirt around his legs. She didn't care. She was well protected in the cocoon of his arms. She leaned her head against his chest, snuggling herself into him, reveling in his warmth.

It all became too much. She wanted to see him, look into that dazzling gaze and view the desire she knew he felt no matter how in control he pretended to be. She turned, an anticipatory smile on her face that quickly dissipated the moment she saw his eyes. She knew he wanted her, but the power of the hunger she saw was unexpected and just a little bit frightening.

Devon tilted her head toward him. He saw his own desire reflected in the green flecks of her eyes. The truth, she'd said. Well, the truth was as clear as the cloudless blue sky above. He wanted her. And she wanted him.

One man and one woman.

No past.

No future.

Just now.

So simple.

When Devon pulled her to him, she didn't protest. When he angled his head and held himself mere millimeters away from her lips, she didn't demur. When he opened his mouth and took hers in a hot, stunning kiss, she responded by touching her tongue to his.

It was all he needed. Like white, hot lightning, desire shot through every cell in his body. He was electrified, on fire, and the wind only fanned it to new heights. He twirled with her in his arms and leaned against the railing so that their bodies were touching in all the right places. She arched into him, melted against his bare chest, wrapped herself around him until he felt every soft curve in contrast to the hardness of his own body.

Devon's lips left hers, wet and eager, to travel down her neck, to the tiny indentation that dipped between her collarbone, and then below. Brazenly he reached down and unbuttoned the first two buttons of her sundress. With one swift movement, her full breasts were exposed to his gaze.

Brooke was dizzy—from his kisses, his heat and the feel of his fingertips on her breasts. He caressed her through her lacy bra, slowly drawing circles around her nipples as he watched with seeming fascination as they swelled and puckered. Then he cupped her breasts in his hands, flicking his thumbs across the tiny orbs with such tenderness that she couldn't stop the whimper from escaping her throat.

"I've wondered—fantasized—about how you would look like this. 'Would she be the same?' I asked myself."

"Am I the same?" she asked, her voice hoarse with desire.

"No. You're not a girl anymore. You're a woman." His mouth returned to hers. "The only thing that's the same is how much I want you."

He kissed her, moving his hands across her shoulders and down her back until he reached her buttocks. He lifted her skirt and cupped her against him. With the tip of one finger he touched her intimately and felt her wet heat through the thin material of her panties. He groaned.

Brooke's knees went weak with the sound, and she wrapped her arms around his neck, threading her fingers through his hair, holding his head in place as she, too, gave herself up to the magic of his mouth and his touch.

They were out of control. Devon felt as if he was inside a hot, roaring volcano about to erupt. He had to get her out of here, preferably to the nearest bed, because if they didn't find one soon, the splintering wood on the deck would have to do.

He broke away, and held her at arm's length. Brooke tightened her grip on his forearms as she caught her breath, knowing full well that if she let go, she'd fall.

Devon rebuttoned her dress. "Let's go inside."

Taking her silence for assent to his unspoken question, Devon led her toward the kitchen door and into the house. She paused midway and looked at him. He saw the flicker of doubt cross her face.

"Don't think," he said.

Biting her lower lip, Brooke decided he was right. This was not a time to think rationally. This was a time to feel, and feel she did, right down to the tingling in her toes.

"Your old bedroom, or mine?"

"Devon—"

Devon kissed her again, silencing her swollen lips with his thumb. "Mine, then."

Brooke let him lead her toward the foyer. His jaw was taut, his face intent, and she knew how tightly he was wound. She felt the same way. Her heart was beating triple time, and her body was throbbing. She should tell him no, but she wouldn't. She wanted him badly... badly enough to throw caution to the wind... badly enough to tuck her suspicions away, if only to spend a little while in the heaven of his arms.

At the foot of the stairway, she stopped, staring at the expanse of steps that led to the bedrooms above. When Devon took the first step, Brooke hesitated. Her heart was beating in her ears, as excitement warred with fear at the thought of making love with him. She felt unsure; it had been so long.

"Come with me, Brooke," he said softly.

As she looked into his eyes, bright blue and glazed with a passion, she remembered the last time he'd spoken those words to her. She had followed him then... Brooke rubbed her arms to ward off a chill, but her hands were soon replaced by Devon's as he pulled her to him.

Devon towered over her. His bare chest heaved with each breath. He took hold of her head in his hands and lifted her face to him. "You know I want you," he said so softly she had to strain to hear him. "But you've got to want me, too." His eyes challenged her. "It's your call, babe."

Brooke stared into his mesmerizing blue eyes, then studied each and every feature of his chiseled face. Such perfection should be illegal, she thought. At the same time, she couldn't stop herself from going up on her tiptoes and offering her mouth to him.

Devon needed no coaxing. He nibbled at her lips, planting small, whisper-kisses around her mouth as he continued to hold her head still. She reached up and touched his chest, threading her fingers through the golden curls, feeling the strong, steady beat of his heart through her palm.

"Oh, yes, baby. Touch me. Touch me all over."

She did. Emboldened by his words, Brooke ran both hands over his chest, up and down, back and forth, until they met in the middle at the snap to his jeans.

"Yes," he whispered harshly against her mouth. "Yes..."

He kissed her then, completely conquering her mouth with his own. She met him halfway as her tongue mated with his. His hands left her head and moved down her arms to her waist. He pulled her up onto the step with him. Their bodies touched, and the contact was electric. The kiss ended. They looked into each other's eyes, communicating more than words ever could. Silently, arm-in-arm, they climbed the stairs.

As they reached the master bedchamber, Devon led her to the four-poster. Brooke sat on the edge of the bed and watched as Devon slowly unsnapped his jeans. Eyes never leaving hers, he pushed first one side down, then the other. He kicked them off, and they landed on the floor in a heap at her feet. He was naked underneath, and fully aroused.

He moved closer to her, leaned over, and kissed her hard on the mouth. "You're next," he said.

Devon stepped back and watched as Brooke took off her sundress. She held it out to him. He took it from her and laid it over the chair near the bed.

"Stand up," he said.

Brooke stood, unselfconscious and proud before him. She was wearing only her lacy bra and matching panties. The day had been too warm for hose, and she had given in to the temptation to feel free and cool. The look in Devon's eyes told her it had been an unexpectedly wise decision.

She took a step toward him and rested her hands on his chest. For the longest moment Devon didn't move a muscle. He couldn't. If he touched her now, he would throw her on the bed and bury himself inside her, no touching, no tasting, no preliminaries of any sort. He was on fire, his arousal straight and high in mute testament to that fact.

"Devon..." Brooke's voice was breathy.

As she rubbed her lips against his chest, he inhaled sharply. "Don't..." he said. "Don't move, not an inch."

Brooke tilted her head back to study him. His look was tight, taut and telling. She felt a surge of feminine power unlike anything she had ever felt before. Ignoring his warning, she ran her hands over his chest once more, then moved down, lower. Boldly she touched the tip of him with her fingers.

Like a cat, she rubbed herself against him, and Devon groaned, grabbing her waist and pulling her hips tightly to him. His head swooped down at the same moment and captured her mouth in a hot, wet, lover's kiss.

They fell on the bed. Devon's hands were all over her, from shoulder to the soft underside of her knee, anywhere and everywhere he could reach. He unsnapped her bra and flung it aside as he caressed and massaged her breasts. He pulled at her nipples, each gentle squeeze in direct concert with the movement of his tongue in her mouth. Brooke felt the tug deep inside her core, alternately seizing and releasing a warm tide of liquid heat.

His mouth replaced his fingers, and soon her breasts were wet with his hungry kisses. She touched his back, his arms, his hair. His skin was on fire, burning on the outside, almost as much as she was burning on the inside.

Devon became impatient. He shimmied her panties down and away, trailing his hand up the inside of her thigh on the return trip. He cupped her between the legs, holding her still when she jumped at the contact.

"Shh," he said. "Let me touch you. Open for me, Brooke. That's it. Open . . ."

Devon threaded his fingers through her damp curls, becoming increasingly more intimate with each caress. When he reached her moist heat, he groaned, and his entire body shuddered. This was what he wanted, had dreamed about for years. A flood of memories engulfed him as he slipped his finger inside her the way he used to so long ago. His body tightened from the memory, and he buried his face into her neck to hide the unexpected emotion it brought in its wake.

Brooke shivered in response. She couldn't take much more of this. She felt as if she were climbing a ladder, going straight up into a blinding light. She was almost there . . . almost . . . and then he found her special place. He touched her with his thumb in slow, firm circles.

Brooke screamed out his name as the ladder crumbled and she felt herself free-fall into a shattering climax.

Devon raised himself on his elbows and looked down into her flushed face. Her eyes were shut tight as if in pain. He knew better. He felt her body tighten under his touch, and the pleasure it gave him was overshadowed only by the distinct pressure of his own need.

Brooke's eyes opened and she gave him a slow smile.

He returned the smile, bent over her and brushed his lips against hers.

"I want to make love with you," he said softly.

Brooke reached down and ran her fingers gently up and down his length. Devon shut his eyes as she wrapped her hand around him. She caressed him slowly, with long, firm strokes until he grabbed hold of her wrist to stop her movements.

"No more," he said.

He reached over Brooke, opened the top drawer on his nightstand, and quickly protected himself. Before she could even comment on his consideration, he was in position between her legs. As she looked up at him, she was sure there had never before been a man so magnificently masculine as this one, poised and ready to make her his own.

And then he did.

Brooke was lost to sensation as he filled her. Each movement of his hips brought him deeper into her body, into her soul. She wrapped her legs around him and met each thrust with a whimper and a sigh. This was what she'd wanted from him from the first. This was what she had always wanted from him. To be his, to be part of him . . . so close, so wonderfully joined, that she couldn't tell where she left off and he began.

Devon was delirious. She was so soft, so tight, so hot, each time his body sank into hers, he was sure he would drown in her loveliness. He lifted her hips to deepen his penetration, but instead of prolonging the pleasure, it only hastened his own release. He tried to stop the roaring in his brain, but his body would have none of it. With a deep, lingering growl, he gave up the fight, and fell over the edge into paradise.

He rested his head on the soft pillow of her breasts while he waited for his heartbeat to return to normal. He felt Brooke kiss his head, then run her fingers through the damp hair at his nape.

For the longest time they just lay there, content, happy, peaceful . . . and, as if by mutual consent, silent. There was too much to say, and words right now would only spoil the beauty of the moment.

The quiet was suddenly shattered by the ringing of the phone. The machine kicked in immediately.

"Hello? Hello? Is anyone there? Devon? Brooke? If anyone's there, please pick up."

Brooke pushed at Devon, and sat up. "It's Chuck."

"Don't answer it," Devon said.

"Well," Chuck's voice continued, "if you're not there, then I'll just leave a message. Where are you two? Lotty can't serve the food until you get here. And everybody's getting pretty darn hungry. Come on, guys, it's party time!"

The machine clicked off.

"Party?" Devon asked. "What party?"

Brooke groaned and held her head in her hands. Devon reached up and pulled her hands from her face. "What party, Brooke?"

"Chuck's party," she said. "The kickoff celebration for the project. Didn't Lotty call you?"

"Yes. She mentioned something about a party, but she chattered away so much I don't remember her saying when it was. It's today?" he asked.

"It's *now*," she said.

Devon looked at her incredulously.

"We figured you forgot all about it. I came to get you."

"And . . . ?"

"*I* forgot."

He gave her a slow smile. "No kidding."

Brooke ignored the warm glow of his smile. She gave him a playful whack on the head. "Let me up," she said.

Brooke grabbed her clothing and ran into the bathroom to freshen up. When she returned, Devon was still lounging naked on the bed.

"Hurry up," she said as she secured her belt. "We're already two hours late for this thing."

"I don't feel like seeing a lot of people right now. Come back to bed."

"Devon, don't be ridiculous. We have to go."

"Why?"

"Because we're expected."

"So?"

"So. If we don't show up, everyone will wonder where we are, what we've been doing. They'll talk."

"I don't care."

Brooke walked over to the bed. Hands on hips, she looked down at his disheveled figure. "I know you don't care. You never *have* cared what people think. But I'm the mayor, and I have to care. Now get up and get dressed."

Devon was annoyed. The last thing he wanted to do was to go to some godawful party and play the "benevolent developer'' game with the townspeople. He was feeling warm, lazy, as if the project and the town were of another time, another place. He had forgotten himself in her arms, and he didn't want to lose that feeling, not yet. But she wasn't going to allow it, and the reality of the situation was returning in full force.

He wasn't ready for that to happen. Swinging his legs over the side of the bed, he beckoned Brooke to him. Hesitantly she came to him. When she was within arm's reach, he pulled her forward to stand between his legs.

"Don't be so uptight, Brooke," he said softly. "We're already two hours late." He toyed with her top button. "What's another hour?"

She slapped his hand away. "Devon, I swear! You are incorrigible." She moved out of his reach, and picked up her purse. Dabbing at her lips with her lipstick, she continued, "As it is, I don't know what I'll tell my brother."

"Tell him the truth," he said, his annoyance clear in his voice. "Tell him you spent the time making love with Devon—in Daddy's bed."

Brooke's hand halted midway to her lips. She stared first at him, then at the bed. It seemed she'd forgotten more than the party; she'd forgotten where she was, and with whom. The familiar four-poster loomed like a great grinning monster of reproach. *Daddy's bed.*

Her lips curled in contempt. "Thank you so much, Devon, for reminding me."

Brooke dropped the lipstick into her purse and snapped it shut. Without another word, she left the room, slamming the door behind her.

"Brooke...damn it," Devon shouted as he jumped from the bed and hopped one-legged into his jeans. "Come back."

She ran down the stairs, and out the door, ignoring his pleas for her to stop. She pulled open her car door and was halfway in when she realized she'd left her keys on the kitchen counter. There was no way she was going back in that house. She'd rather walk first. Slamming the car door, she marched past his Jaguar right out onto Dune Road. Her heels crunched in the dirt, but her pace never lessened as she headed in the direction of Chuck's house.

It didn't matter, she told herself, what he thought of her. It didn't matter one bit whatever the reason he'd taken her to bed. She'd enjoyed it, right? That's all that mattered. So what if all Devon wanted was to prove he could seduce her.

So he could.

Easily.

Big deal.

Perhaps he needed to satisfy some warped feelings he had toward her father. That was okay. She could handle it. She'd handled worse.

It had been her decision. He hadn't forced her. She was an adult, and it was her prerogative to go to bed with whomever she wanted, wasn't it? She certainly wasn't going to feel ashamed of what she did.

She was a big girl, and like the old song said, big girls don't cry. Right? Right.

Determinedly, Brooke put one foot in front of the other, trying her best to ignore the hot tears of frustration, anger and hurt welling up in her eyes.

Seven

"Get in the car."

"Go to hell."

"Brooke. Get in the car."

She ignored him and kept walking. Devon lifted his foot from the brake and let the car coast. He spoke to her through the open passenger side door, which swayed precariously with each dip in the road.

"What do you want me to say?" Devon asked. "You want me to say I'm sorry? Okay. I'm sorry I made that crack about your father. Now get in the car."

"Drop dead."

"Brooke, don't make me get out of the car. You won't like it."

"I'm scared to death," she said.

Devon muttered an expletive. "Get in the damn car!"

Brooke stopped. Devon braked.

"I'm not getting in the car with you. I'm not going anywhere with you ever again. Is that perfectly clear?"

"Yes," he said. "Now, get in and we'll discuss it."

She began walking again. "There's nothing to discuss. I hate you."

He followed her. "Since when?"

"Since always."

"You sure have a funny way of showing it," he said, amusement evident in his voice.

"I don't have to like you to make love with you," she said.

"Oh, no?"

"No."

"So, you've become a woman of the world now, right?"

"Right."

He laughed. Brooke stopped and poked her head inside the car.

"Go away," she said.

"No. Get in the ca—"

The sound of a blasting horn interrupted them. Brooke recognized the approaching station wagon, and her stomach dropped into a free-fall. She quickly jumped into the passenger seat and shut the door.

"It's Chuck."

Mumbling another, more descriptive expletive, Devon stopped at the side of the road. Chuck pulled up next to them.

"Where have you two been? I've been all over town looking for you," Chuck shouted through the open window. "What happened, Brooke? Why so late?"

Brooke leaned forward, hoping her brother couldn't see her flushed face from this distance. "We were just on our way. Something came up that couldn't wait."

"I'll say," Devon said.

Brooke punched Devon's arm to keep him quiet as she spoke to her brother. "We'll follow you, Chuck."

Chuck waved his assent and took off. When Devon didn't immediately follow, Brooke said, "Will you please follow him?"

Devon's crystal-blue gaze held her fast. Defiantly, she refused to look away.

"This isn't finished," he said.

He peeled out, leaving a trail of pebbles and dust in his wake. They drove in silence to Chuck's house. The party was well under way, and they were soon separated by the press of people wanting Devon's attention. Brooke watched him work the room like a seasoned politician, shaking hands and making himself available to each and every citizen who wished to talk to him.

The night seemed endless. She allowed herself to be drawn into a debate about whether or not to have a parade during Octoberfest. She offered little to the conversation, smiled until her face hurt, and then smiled some more because she had to. It was a great cover-up for how she really felt—edgy, restless, and thoroughly self-conscious. She felt as if she had a neon sign blinking across her forehead in colored lights: I Spent The Afternoon In Bed With Devon Taylor.

Lotty served the food, but Brooke couldn't eat a thing. Her insides felt as if they were being progressively churned by every speed a blender had to offer—mix, chop, grate—and whenever Devon looked at her—liquefy.

She followed him with her eyes. She couldn't help it. Each time their gazes connected they would communicate before moving on. She told herself she hated him, hated his smart mouth, hated whatever it was he was planning to do to the town, to the bank, to her. But it wasn't true. She didn't hate him. And that was the problem.

It had been easier before to pretend, before she had felt his arms, his touch, before she felt him move inside her. Now, with each look, she relived each sensation, and her body reacted to the promise in his eyes— "This isn't finished," he'd said. Her pulse jumped with the prospect. She alternately dreaded and hungered for it.

Brooke felt as if he were stalking her, like a predator and his prey, yet he hadn't made a move toward her all evening. It was her own guilty conscience, she decided, that made her feel this way. What must he think of her? A kiss, a caress, and she'd fallen into bed with him.

She'd thought she was long over him, but obviously such was not the case. There were still feelings deep down that had never been dealt with. And now they were all surfacing, fast and furiously. She was frightened by what she saw in his eyes, but more so by what she felt in her heart.

She wanted to be near him; she wanted to run away. Tonight, for completely different reasons, neither was possible.

Devon watched her, but kept his distance. Lord knew he wanted to be close to her, to hold her hand, to touch her skin, to wrap an arm around her waist. He didn't dare. If he touched her again, it would be all over. Her throbbing energy called out to him, and his body homed in on it.

He could still smell her woman's scent on himself. It made him feel charged, wild, and it was all he could do to hold still and answer people's questions when all he really wanted to do was escape the confines of the room, these people, the very clothes on his body—anything that separated him from Brooke.

He glanced out the window. Night had fallen and soon he could take Brooke and leave. He would have to coax her, he knew. The remark about Chaz's bed had been a cheap shot, stupid, uncalled for. He had let his need for revenge spoil a perfect day of love. The thought twisted inside of him, causing confusion and uncertainty.

This was what he had hungered for, this perfect revenge—Brooke in his bed and the bank in the palm of his hand. Everything was working out so well, it seemed preordained and blessed by the gods. But his feelings were turning out to be the wild card in this whole plan. He didn't *want* to feel anything...not for the town, nor for any Pattersen, especially not Brooke.

But he did. When they'd made love this afternoon, his mind had turned to mush, and his body had taken control. There had been no thought of revenge, only the joy and pure pleasure of being joined to her. He'd lost himself—and his need for vengeance—in the softness and sweetness of her flesh.

That had bothered him, he realized now, more than he had admitted. That vulnerability had produced the snide remark about her father. He'd had a need to chop her down to size, to put her in her place, and for what? Because she had gotten to him. Big time.

Devon took a sip of beer. He stared at Brooke over the rim of the can. As if he'd called out to her, she turned. Her eyes were a window to her soul tonight, and tonight, they spoke of a need as basic and powerful as his own. Her look tormented him, made his body ache, but more than that, it haunted him.

Once was not enough. A thousand times would not be enough.

Brooke read the message loud and clear. She had to get out of here, had to get away from his relentless eyes. She needed space, air. Diplomatically she extricated herself from a heated discussion on the merits of copper sewage piping versus PVC, and headed for the kitchen to find her brother. She pushed at the swinging door and poked her head inside.

"Lotty, where's Chuck?" she asked.

Her sister-in-law was adding cheese and crackers to a picked-at platter and didn't look up. "Out back, I think. With Harry Nelson. Now don't you go riling him up."

"I don't rile Chuck," Brooke said.

"Yes, you do. He's always upset when he talks to you. Then I have to soothe things over."

"But you do that so well, Lotty."

"You have a real fresh mouth, Brooke. Sad thing you didn't have a mama to wash it out with soap."

"Is that what your mother did to you?" Brooke asked as she picked up a carrot stick.

"My mama didn't have to. *I* was a lady through and through."

Brooke remembered Lotty as a young girl with her white gloves and matching shoes and bag, and had to agree. She was a lady. Never gave anyone a bit of trouble. Unlike some people she knew.

"Well, Lotty, we all can't be as perfect as you."

Lotty peeked around the door frame. "You watch yourself with that one," she said with a nod of her head.

Brooke didn't have to ask who she meant. Or what she meant, for that matter. "I can handle Devon."

Lotty made a disparaging sound. "Like you handled him before? Just make sure you don't fall in that same trap again this time 'round."

"Thanks for the advice, Lotty, but I know what I'm doing," she said, wondering if that were indeed true.

Brooke let the door swing shut and headed out into the backyard. Chuck was deep in conversation with Harry as he stood by the barbecue flipping hamburgers. She sidled up to him and joined in. The night air was cool, but it felt good against her fevered skin. She linked her arm through Chuck's, and breathed a sigh of relief.

Devon surveyed the room for Brooke, and caught a glimpse of her in the kitchen with Lotty. He grabbed a fresh can of beer from the cooler and followed her, but stopped short when he saw her in the midst of a conversation with Chuck and Harry Nelson, the contractor they had chosen to do the work on the condo-tel.

Harry's presence pierced through the cloud of desire that engulfed Devon. It brought the project back to mind in full force. The bids had come in quickly for the construction work on the project. They were low bids, too, clean, close-to-the-bone bids that under other circumstances would have set Devon's juices flowing in anticipation of the competitive bargaining.

But there had been no time for bargaining here. Devon needed to get the work started while everyone was still enamored with the plan, with him. Any day someone could discover a chink that would call a halt to the entire project.

He couldn't let that happen. Chuck Pattersen had just yesterday signed away his bank and his life. It was so close now, Devon could almost taste it. He leaned against the door and observed the little group as he took a swig of beer. Some might say he was perpetrating fraud, but he knew better. Everything he was doing was perfectly legal, though he made good use of every available loophole the law had to offer.

This wasn't fraud; it was justice. And it was long overdue.

Chuck drew Brooke into the crook of his arm and gave her an affectionate squeeze. The sight disturbed Devon, an unwelcome reminder that she was one of *them*. As sure as he was about the project, he was as equally unsure as to what was happening to him and Brooke. This questioning of himself, his motives, was something he had never done before. Part of him didn't want her touched by, or even involved in the project. The other, more logical side of him was single-minded in his need for revenge against each and every Pattersen. But his desire for her was clouding his line of right and wrong.

He wanted her physically, but he was also sure he could remain detached from her emotionally. He watched as she laughed with Chuck. She *was* part of them. No matter how pliable she became in his arms, no matter how she responded to his touch, no matter how much he wanted to bury himself inside her, she was now—as she had always been—his enemy.

He chided himself. He wouldn't let the passion between them affect his plan. Sharing his bed was not the same as sharing his thoughts, mind...heart. He dismissed the feelings of protectiveness that washed over him. That was just a by-product of his desire. It had nothing to do with the deep-down need he'd once felt for her. Wanting and needing were two different things.

Weren't they?

A surge of unwelcome anger overcame him. It was directed at himself, not Brooke, which made it all the more potent. He would not allow her to do it again—to insinuate herself into his life, to get under his skin, to weave her sensual web around him so that his thinking became distorted.

Was that what she was doing this afternoon? Why had she made love with him? Was it part of her plan to sabotage him, to cut him off at the knees? He had become entangled in her web before, and she had been much younger then. What was she capable of now? For all he knew, she could be purposely using her body to get to him.

He remembered the night when he'd made dinner and that dress she'd worn. The thought disturbed him, but also cleared his head, putting everything back in its proper perspective. It could be true. He knew from experience that the Pattersens would use everything and anything they had to accomplish what they wanted.

"Devon! Come on over here," Chuck said. "Harry and I were just discussing phase one. His crew will be out at the site on Monday."

"You're not wasting any time," Brooke said cautiously.

"Why should we?" Devon asked her.

The warmth was gone from his eyes, replaced by an icy, challenging look. Brooke opened her mouth to comment, then changed her mind. What had happened in the space of a few minutes to turn him from hot to cold?

"No reason," she said. "If everything's ready."

"Everything's ready," Devon said. "The sooner we start, the sooner we finish."

"And the sooner we sell them!" Chuck said.

The edge of nervousness in her brother's voice brought back the enormity of the bank's investment. Brooke shivered, whether from the cool night air or the direction of her thoughts, she wasn't sure.

"Cold?" Devon asked.

"A little."

He shrugged out of his jacket and placed it over her shoulders.

"Thanks," she said.

"Are you ready?" he asked.

"Ready?"

"To leave," he said.

"So soon?" Chuck asked.

"Got to," Devon answered. "Busy day tomorrow. I'm fixing up the dock."

"Oh, then I won't bother you," Brooke said politely, grateful for such an easy way out. "I'll pick up my car later. I can get a ride from someone else."

"No bother." His voice was noncommittal, but his eyes issued a challenge.

Brooke felt the heat rise again.

"Go ahead, then," Chuck said to Brooke. "Stop by tomorrow to help us finish up all this food. Harry? Keep an eye on the grill while I walk them out."

After a steady stream of goodbyes, Devon and Brooke made their way through the house and out to the car. As she slipped into the front seat of his Jaguar, Brooke heard her brother mumble something to Devon. They rode in strained silence until Devon reached his house. Brooke followed him inside and picked up her keys from the kitchen counter, but didn't dawdle. He seemed so intense and distracted that she was surprised when he walked her back out to her car.

"What did Chuck say to you?" she asked, breaking the silence.

"He said he was happy to see us on speaking terms."

"That's all?"

Devon shrugged. "And that maybe you were mellowing."

"Mellowing?"

"His word, not mine," Devon said.

"Am I?" she asked.

"No."

"You don't think I'm mellowing toward you?"

"No."

"Then what do you call what happened today?" she asked.

"I have no idea, Brooke. What the hell did happen today?"

"We made love."

"Did we?"

"I thought so."

"Then answer me this," he said. "Why?"

"Why did we make love?"

"Why did *you* make love with *me?*"

Brooke felt the blood rise to her face. "Because . . . I wanted to."

"No ulterior motive?"

"What possible ulterior motive could I have?"

Devon laughed derisively. "Maybe the same one you had the first time."

"Devon, I don't know what you're getting at, but if you have something to say, I'd appreciate you just coming out with it."

Devon gave her a long, hard stare. His eyes sparkled like blue diamonds in the night.

"All right," he said finally. "You used sex to get rid of me once before. You can't blame me for thinking you might use it again for the same reason."

Brooke stared at him incredulously. She couldn't believe her ears. Was he trying to say that he didn't run away, that she *drove* him away the first time?

"I think you've lost your mind," she said. "I never 'used sex' with you, ever. I loved you, Devon."

"You didn't know the first thing about love, babe."

That was it. What had begun as a ripple of anger was fast becoming a tidal wave. "And *you* did?" she asked, enraged.

The churning in Brooke's stomach was almost more than she could bear. She wasn't going to take this, not from him. She pulled open her car door and got in in such a hurry that the strap from her purse became entangled with the door handle. Rage and humiliation battled for first place in her mind. Rage won.

"You say I didn't know anything about love? Well, Devon Taylor, if that's true, you're worse than me. Because you were—are—*incapable* of love. You never loved anything or anyone in your life. Especially not me, not ever." She swallowed the tears stuck in her throat. "Love. You have a nerve even using the word in front of me."

Brooke threw his jacket at him, slammed the door, and sped away.

Devon climbed the steps as he watched her weaving taillights disappear. He shut his eyes, took a deep breath, and slowly banged his forehead against the door frame.

"Well, you handled that well," he said out loud to himself, then recalled her words. He shook his head. "You're wrong about that, babe. Dead wrong. I *did* know how to love. Especially you."

_____

_____

_____

_____

Eight

————

"This is it."

Brooke stared down at the carton filled with papers and file folders. "All of it?" she asked.

"Everything Chuck had to offer," her assistant, Joan, answered.

Brooke took a deep breath, and checked her watch. It was after four o'clock in the afternoon, and she had already put in a full day.

"Should we start now?" she asked.

"Okay by me," Joan said. "Wally's going bowling tonight. I don't have to cook dinner. If you need me to stay late, you've got me."

Brooke squeezed Joan's arm. "You're a doll. And you've got a deal." She pushed up her sleeves. "Let's get started."

Each of the women picked a thick file folder from the carton and headed for their respective desks. Brooke turned to page one and scrutinized it, then flipped through several other pages until she found an item worth a double look—a letter of intent from one of Devon's investors. She pulled the letter out and set it aside.

After about an hour or so, the stack of "later" papers had grown to a sizable mound. Brooke leaned back in her chair and rubbed her neck. She glanced out the window. It was dark, and the wind was picking up. Most of the lights in the shops on Main Street were dimmed as the businesses closed for the night.

"How's it going?" she called to Joan.

"Slow," Joan answered.

Brooke stood and walked into the anteroom to Joan's desk. "Find anything interesting?"

"No, not really. Everything looks pretty straightforward. It would help if I knew what we were looking for."

Brooke sighed. "I wish I knew. This is just a hunch, Joan. I don't know what there is in these folders, but I just *feel* there is something we don't know about Maiden Point." She pointed to the papers strewn across Joan's desk. "But I'll bet money the answer is somewhere in here."

Brooke drifted back into her office and began sorting through papers once again. She suppressed a yawn. This had been an extremely long day, and it was getting longer by the minute.

The day after Chuck's party, she had approached him about releasing the bank's files on Maiden Point. He had balked, of course, insulted that she was questioning his ability to investigate the project. After much cajoling and reassuring that such was not the case, Chuck had complied with her request, but it had taken him almost two weeks to gather all the information she'd requested.

And what a two weeks it had been. She and Devon were barely on speaking terms—mostly her doing. She was angry and hurt. His outrageous remarks that night replayed themselves over and over in her mind. To accuse *her* of using *him* was self-deception of the highest order. It amazed her that his conscience would even allow him to justify the thought after what he'd done to her.

Making love with him had been a gigantic mistake. With each touch, each caress, she had exposed another little piece of herself, until she had left herself wide open to any and every device Devon wished to use against her. He was a master at turning someone else's weakness to his advantage, and she had fallen willingly into his trap.

Brooke knew she only had herself to blame. After all, what had she expected? Hearts and flowers? From Devon? What a laugh!

To give him credit for some modicum of sensitivity, he had tried to talk to her since then, but she'd been avoiding him like the plague. It was a self-protective measure that seemed not only wise but necessary. He had soon gotten the message and had stopped trying to contact her. But she knew he had not given up. That wasn't Devon's style. He was probably retrenching, hoping to catch her in another weak moment.

So, she'd made a mistake. She had made them before, and no doubt would again. She had paid for each and every one of them, and this would be no different. She had to be cool, aloof, reserved where Devon was concerned, and that meant she couldn't be alone with him . . . because Lord knew what happened to her then.

When all was said and done, even their sweet interlude in bed didn't dilute the deep distrust she had for him and this project.

It had been on that very night that she'd decided to do something about it. She needed to take an active role, to feel as if she were accomplishing something, to give her some sort of control where Devon was concerned.

She hadn't counted on Chuck's being so ornery about helping out. Precious time had passed, and she still had no notion as to what she was looking for. The work on the condo-tel was moving along at a very rapid pace. It seemed much of the preliminary inner work had already been completed, and the model was near ready to open. Chuck was chomping at the bit to show it to the general public, hoping to arouse enough interest in the off-season to insure successful sales in the spring.

Joan poked her head into the office. "How about some coffee?"

Brooke rolled her head back and forth. "No thanks, Joan. I've already had too much today."

"Why don't you leave?" Joan said. "You look beat. And tomorrow's a busy day. Go on home, take a hot bath, and get a good night's sleep."

Brooke smiled at her colleague and friend. "Yes, Mother," she said. "It does sound like a good idea. For both of us. Why don't you pack it in, too?"

"I will in a little while. Why don't you leave your papers with me? I'll go over them, then I'll leave."

Brooke lifted her pocketbook out of the bottom drawer of her desk. She paused by Joan on her way out to hand her the stack of papers she had set aside for further review. "Here they are. I doubt you'll find anything. Don't stay too late."

"I won't. Tomorrow's an early day."

"Isn't it ever," Brooke said, and headed out the door.

Octoberfest was to begin bright and early the next morning, and Brooke wasn't looking forward to it. Lenape Bay had instituted the festival several years ago as a means of generating off-season business for the shops and restaurants in town. As mayor, it was Brooke's duty to give a short speech to start things off, which, for the first time this year, included a parade. She had thought the whole idea a bit pretentious, but had been overruled by the majority.

As Brooke turned down Dune Road, her heart sank in her chest. Devon would be there, too—right next to her, in fact, for he was the guest of honor and grand marshal for the day. She had given up her protests, hadn't even bothered to voice her concerns about him any longer. He was everyone's darling right now, and she was the shrew—the woman scorned who couldn't get over the past.

So tomorrow morning, Devon Taylor and Brooke Wallace would stand shoulder to shoulder, smile, and wave as they led the group down Main Street. She shook her head at the absurdity of the situation. For all appearances they would seem the best of friends, the most trusted of colleagues, while on the inside they'd be seething with unresolved feelings for each other.

She passed the old Victorian house and noted that Devon's car was in the driveway. The lights were on in the parlor, but she could see no movement within. She sped by, not even slowing for a better look. Brooke rounded the bend and pulled into her own driveway. She breathed a sigh of relief. It was good to be home. She rushed inside. Without any preliminaries, she changed her clothes and ran a hot, steaming bath. While waiting for the tub to fill, she laid down logs and started a fire.

The weather had turned cool the morning after Chuck's party. Indian summer had abruptly disappeared, and the temperature dropped twenty degrees in one day. Most evenings, Brooke lit a fire, wanting to preserve the feeling of natural warmth as long as possible, dreading the long winter of artificial furnace heat.

For the longest time, she lay in the tub, clearing her mind of all thought, almost falling asleep. When the water cooled enough to be uncomfortable, she drained it, wrapped a clean, white towel around her head and donned a white terry cloth robe. She brewed a cup of herb tea and wandered into her living room. Turning out all the lights, she sat on the sofa and stared into the flames.

Brooke checked the clock on the mantel. It was only ten o'clock. Too early for bed. Should she watch TV or read? She couldn't summon the will to make a decision. She opted instead to turn on the radio. She found a soft rock station, sighed as she put her feet up, and sipped her tea. Just for a little while, she thought, and sank back into the sofa. Just for a little while...

Within minutes she was asleep.

Devon knocked lightly on the patio door. There was no answer, but he could see the dim glow from the fireplace reflecting itself in the glass. He tapped again, then decided to let himself in. The door was locked, but as was the case with these old sliders, it didn't take a professional thief to trip the latch.

He found her asleep on the couch, the fire waning, light music filling the room with background noise. For a long time, Devon just stood, watching her, wondering if he should take his leave and let her sleep. Instead he moved closer. She looked so peaceful. Her skin had a well-scrubbed glow. Her clean scent filled his nostrils as he bent over her, and his body tightened instantly in response.

He shouldn't be here. But she had been avoiding him, refusing his phone calls, and being outright hostile to him in public. Tomorrow was the damned Octoberfest, and he would have to be part of it. So would she. He needed a show of support, not contempt from her, and that's why he'd decided on a confrontation tonight instead of tomorrow morning.

At least that was the reason he gave himself for showing up here at this hour.

Devon had been in the city all day. He'd spent more time thinking about Brooke than about the business at hand. The entire ride back to the shore had been dedicated to analyzing each and every step he'd taken with her since his return.

He hadn't liked the results of his self-examination. He had to admit that he hadn't treated her well. He was blaming Brooke for his reaction to her, and that didn't appeal to his sense of justice. Regardless of what she'd done to him in the past, it was clear that they were linked in some primordial way that had nothing to do with her connection to the Pattersens or his vendetta against them.

There was an intangible *something* between the two of them that transcended all the problems, that brought them both back to basics whenever they were alone together. Call it chemistry, call it lust, he didn't know *what* to call it. All he did know was that it was deeply embedded in his soul . . . and powerful enough to wake him up in the middle of the night and send him to her.

There was a chill in the air, and Devon placed another log on the fire. It slipped and a few sparks spat out onto the rug. He stomped on them with the heel of his shoe, and as he turned, he saw her eyes on him, opened and staring. He returned her stare, unspeaking, wondering if she were awake or in the middle of a dream.

"Who...?"

She was awake.

"Me."

"How did you get in?"

"I popped the lock. I wanted to talk to you."

"You what...?" Brooke glanced at the clock. Two a.m. She pushed herself up on one elbow. "Now?"

The towel shifted on her head into a lopsided turban. Devon reached over and unraveled it. It was damp. He rolled it into a ball and threw it in the corner, then sat beside her on the edge of the couch.

"I couldn't sleep," he said.

Brooke's robe gaped open, revealing a creamy curve of her breast. Without a second thought, Devon reached inside and caressed her. Brooke grabbed hold of his wrist to stop him. She had to. She wasn't awake, and her resistance was low. She wasn't quite ready to react to the joy she suddenly felt at seeing him, let alone to the fact that his dry, warm touch had set her heart thumping.

It felt too good to let him continue.

"What do you want to talk about?"

Devon removed his hand from inside her robe, but instead of moving away from her, he threaded his fingers through her still-damp hair and combed them through.

"About tomorrow."

He began to massage her scalp.

Brooke shut her eyes as tingles of sensation swept over her. "Wh-what about tomorrow?"

His other hand joined the first. Like an affectionate kitten, Brooke moved her head to the rhythm of his hands.

"The parade," he said softly as he continued his massage. "We need to talk."

His words registered, and she nodded inwardly. They did need to talk. Brooke reached up, making a conscious decision to push him away, but when her hand touched the hard muscles of his chest and felt the strong beat of his heart, she failed to push at all. Instead she began to move her hand in slow, sensual circles.

"Talk," she said, or tried to—her voice cracked and betrayed her state of mind.

In one swift motion, Devon pulled his hooded sweatshirt over his head. He took hold of her hand and placed it back onto the center of his chest. "Don't stop," he said.

Brooke's second hand joined her first, roaming freely over his bare muscles. She found his flat nipple and flicked her finger across it. His sharp intake of breath brought her eyes to his.

"I thought you wanted to talk," she said softly.

"Later."

He kissed her. She let him. When his tongue brushed against her lips, she opened her mouth for him. At first he tasted cool, then very warm, slightly minty, and deliciously Devon. Brooke began to tremble.

He broke away and trailed hot, wet kisses across her neck, down past her collarbone, to the raised tips of her breasts, which he licked and nipped and suckled until they were tight, wet, pouting peaks. He parted her robe.

She was naked underneath, and his crystal eyes glowed in the darkness as his hand trailed down between her breasts to her soft, round belly. He stopped just short of the one spot that ached to be touched.

"You are so beautiful. So soft and beautiful."

"Devon..." she said.

"Hmm..."

"We shouldn't."

"No, we shouldn't," he agreed. He brushed the backs of his knuckles against her chestnut curls.

"You should leave," she said, but even as the words left her lips, her legs parted to give him better access.

"You're right. I should."

Devon touched her intimately. His fingers delved into her warmth, and she gasped for breath as she felt herself close around them. He moved back and forth across her sensitive flesh with a slow, steady rhythm that opened a floodgate of liquid heat. With each deft stroke, she became more slick and swollen with desire.

Devon watched her face as she writhed beneath his hand. His eyes were a blazing blue, and they held hers in a mesmerizing gaze.

"Tell me to go away," he said.

Brooke swallowed audibly, running her hands from his chest up to his neck, pulling him closer to her. "Go away," she whispered.

Without missing a beat, Devon undid his pants. "Say it like you mean it."

Brooke ran her hands down his belly and tugged at his zipper. She reached into his waistband, and touched him. He was achingly hard... and so very hot.

She swallowed. "Go... away."

Her hand closed around his thickness, and Devon's entire body stiffened. Unable to stand the constraints of his clothing, he rose, and undressed, discarding his pants in a heap by the fire. He stood before her, naked and proud, a perfect specimen of the aroused male in all his glory.

Devon held out his hand to her. She took it and allowed him to help her up from the couch. Her robe fell off her shoulders and hung on to her forearms.

"Stay or go, Brooke? Tell me what you want."

Brooke's insides shook. What was the point? From the moment she'd opened her eyes and seen him standing there, the decision had already been made, hadn't it?

"Stay," she whispered as she let the robe fall to the floor. "I want you, Devon. All of you."

Devon took her into his arms and held her to him. They dropped to their knees, bodies straining to get as close as possible—closer. He held her head as his lips brushed each and every feature of her face before settling at her mouth. He started slowly, first nibbling at her lower lip, then tracing the tip of his tongue against her upper until she parted her lips in open invitation.

She touched her tongue to his, and at that moment the thin thread of control he had been nurturing finally snapped. His kisses became wild, hot and deep. A small voice in the back of his mind keep reminding him to slow down, to take it easy, but it was no use. The sweetness of her mouth overwhelmed him, blotting out all thoughts, all excuses.

This was the real reason he'd awakened from a deep sleep, the reason his blood pumped erratically through his veins whenever he so much as said her name, the reason he was compelled to venture out in the middle of the night and break down her door if necessary to see her.

Yes, he wanted to talk to her, but he also wanted to taste her, feel her, smell her, absorb her into himself if it were at all possible to do so.

His hands left her face, skimmed down her spine and cupped her buttocks against him.

"Oh, baby, feel me," he whispered.

"I do," Brooke said, her voice muffled by his chest as he held her tightly. She rolled her head back to look at him. "I want to touch you, too, Devon. I want..."

Devon's face softened as her words trailed off. His body gradually relaxed. "What do you want? Tell me."

Brooke looked away from his penetrating eyes. She felt embarrassed all of a sudden, which, under the circumstances was utterly ridiculous.

"I don't know what you want me to say," she said.

Devon placed his hands at her waist, and pulled her down onto the rug. "Your fantasies," he said. "You do have some, don't you?"

"Everyone does."

"So..."

Devon stretched out on his back with his hands under his head. The fire cast a golden glow to his body. Brooke looked him over, from the top of his head all the way down to the tip of his toes. Her eyes glazed as a few very personal, secret thoughts ricocheted through her mind. Her face flushed.

Devon watched the wheels in her mind spin. He grinned his infamous half-smirk. "Go for it, babe. I'm all yours."

Brooke's hazel eyes darkened to the color of whiskey. She leaned over him, gently brushing her lips against his. He didn't move. She kissed his cheeks, his eyes, the slight dip in his chin. And still he didn't move.

"You'll stay still?" she asked.

"If that's what you want," he said.

"Promise?"

Linking his hands securely behind his head, he asked, "That good enough?"

Brooke smiled. Emboldened by her new power over him, she placed one hand on either side of his chest and straddled him. Devon gave her a slow grin, but said nothing. He looked as though he was truly enjoying himself. That was fine with her. So was she.

With slow, teasing caresses, she lightly stroked him, feeling the texture of his skin under the curly hair on his chest. She followed the track as it narrowed down in a direct path to where their bodies met. His stomach muscles flexed as her hand moved lower, but, as promised, he didn't move.

Brooke leaned forward and kissed him deeply. Her lips left his and followed the same route as her hands, covering every inch of his chest as she tasted her way down his body. His skin was hot to the touch, taut and smooth. It excited her to rub her face against each spot before moving on to the next.

She stopped her trail of kisses just above his sex, then rested her head against his thigh. She didn't touch him at all. Instead she blew her warm breath against him, watching as his body became more aroused with each breath. It pleased her to feel his thigh muscles tighten in an attempt to maintain control, and she continued her airy assault, until he brought his knee up.

"I thought you weren't going to move?" she teased.

"Sorry," he said, and lowered his leg back to its original position.

Brooke gave in to temptation and reached out and took him into her hand. She stroked him completely, up, down, around and under. He was like velvet, his flesh hot and heavy in her hand. She knew he was on fire; she could feel the tension in his body. But she, too, was aroused. The pleasure she was giving him was coming back to her tenfold. Touching him, feeling his reaction to her manifest itself so strongly, was making her heart beat faster, and her body quickened with a need as urgent as his own.

All of a sudden it wasn't enough to touch him any longer. Her lips replaced her hand, and she gloried in her own ability to throw off all her inhibitions and enjoy him as fully as she had ever dreamed. He was such a beautiful man, and despite all that they'd been through together, there was no one else on earth she would want to share a moment like this with. With tears in her eyes, she took him into her mouth.

Devon's body began to shake. His hands had long ago left the safety of behind his head. He was now gripping the carpet fibers, digging his nails into them in a vain attempt not to pull her up and bury himself inside her. It had seemed a great idea at the time, but promising not to touch her was driving him crazy. And her mouth...no, don't think about what she was doing, he told himself. Think about tomorrow, think about the bank, think about...

He muttered an expletive, and groped around the floor for his pants. He quickly retrieved the foil packet before pulling Brooke up over him. He grabbed her hair to hold her head still, then took her mouth with a wide-open, starving-man's kiss. He was trembling with desire, but he couldn't stop it. He didn't give a damn, either. He was safe. He was with Brooke.

Devon lifted her by the waist and settled her directly on top of him. With one deep thrust, he was inside her. She was so hot, so wet, so ready for him, he had to shut his eyes and keep perfectly still for the longest minute to gain what little bit of control he could grasp before he lost himself again.

Brooke leaned into him. She placed one hand on either side of his head. She stared into his eyes of blue fire. "You broke your promise," she whispered.

Devon looked up at her. Her hair was a gorgeous, tangled mess, her lips were swollen, and her face had the look of a woman ready for passion.

"Sue me."

He kissed her, thrusting up into her at the same time. Brooke groaned her acceptance of him into his mouth and moved with him. His hands were all over her, caressing everywhere within reach. When he gently rubbed and tugged on her nipples, her insides reacted in kind. It was all becoming too much. She quickened her pace and took him deeper into her. She was close, so close...

Devon reached down between their bodies and touched her, drawing slow, intimate circles with the pad of his thumb. Her body began to shake, and he could feel the spasms take her...and him over the edge. Even as his body gave itself over to the pleasure of the moment, he fought to hold off, to make it last longer. But he couldn't. This was Brooke's show, and she had called the shots from beginning to end.

And he'd loved every minute of it.

He pulled her close to him and rocked her in his arms. After a moment he felt her shoulders move ever so slightly.

"Are you cold?" he asked.

She shook her head.

"Brooke?" he asked, then pulled back to see her face.

She was crying. Tears streaked down her face. His stomach clenched, and his chest felt as if he'd been whacked with a tire iron. The sight knocked him for a loop.

"What's wrong?"

"Nothing."

"Don't tell me nothing. Did I hurt you?"

"No."

"Then why the hell are you crying?"

"Devon, don't..."

"Don't what? Don't ask?" He sat up and pulled her along with him. "Why the hell are you crying?"

"I don't know. I just feel like crying."

He stroked her face. "Why, babe? Tell me why?"

She looked into his eyes and new tears began. "It was so beautiful, wasn't it?" she whispered.

Devon knew she was talking about what they had just shared. He nodded. "Yeah. It was beautiful." Long-suppressed feelings surfaced. He tried to push them away, but unlike in the past, he wasn't successful. Cradling her in his arms, he leaned against the couch and shut his eyes. "It always is with us."

For the longest time, they held each other. Brooke dried her eyes and rested her head on his chest. She stared at the dying embers. The fire had lost its original fierceness and was now a mixture of ash and glowing cinder. Just like us, Brooke thought, all hot and raging at the beginning, all mixed up and undecided at the end.

"I *did* love you, Devon," she said softly into the darkness. "Tell me you believe me."

Devon fought the emotions whirring around inside of his head. He didn't want to dredge up those old feelings. It was bad enough he couldn't keep his hands off her. He didn't want to think about Brooke in terms of love, not love then...nor love now. Yet he couldn't deny the impact her words had on him.

The music played softly in the background. "Yesterday" by the Beatles. How apropos, he thought, and tightened his hold on her.

"I believe you," he said.

And the worst part of it all was that he did.

Nine

Brooke surveyed Main Street through her office window. It was certainly a fine day for a parade. Come to think of it, there had probably never been a finer day in all creation. Wasn't the sky just a tad bluer? The sun a bit brighter? Or did it just look that way after a night of sublime madness, an erotic night that seemed to go on forever? There were more questions than answers in her mind today. The only thing she was sure of was that she'd never felt more alive.

She had arrived bright and early at the office. Mainly because she had been up bright and early. Mainly because she'd barely slept at all.

Last night was still both vivid and unreal. She had never had such an experience. Making love was something you did once, maybe twice, but all night long? She covered her face with her hands. After fulfilling her own personal fantasy, Devon fulfilled a few of his own.

They'd worked their way through every room in her house and ended up in her bed by dawn.

Brooke stretched. Wound tight from lack of sleep, she was sore in some very new and interesting places. A Cheshire-cat smile graced her lips as tiny flashes of last night skipped through her mind, reminders of how each delicious ache was acquired. Her furniture would never look the same to her.

A change had overtaken her, not just physically, but mentally, too. Her attitude toward Devon had taken a decided turn toward ambivalence. It wasn't as if she still didn't have doubts about him—no amount of love-making could completely obliterate that—but she'd be lying to herself if she didn't admit that what they shared last night had dramatically altered her perceptions.

Only yesterday she was combing through the Maiden Point files searching for any obscure clue as proof against him. Today, she questioned her motives for doing so. Was Chuck right? Was she being unreasonable? Was the past clouding the present, sabotaging the future?

The night had been emotionally charged. She had laughed with him, cried with him, done things to him and with him that she had never seriously considered acting out in reality. He had come over to "talk" he'd said, but talk was the one thing they hadn't even attempted. It was as if communicating with their bodies was less intimate—and less dangerous—than doing so with their minds.

Nothing seemed clear this morning. Brooke told herself it was to be expected. A woman couldn't spend a night like that with a man and come away unchanged. At least, not a woman like her.

Yawning, she checked her watch, then muttered to herself. She was late. She grabbed her jacket off the hook on the back of her office door, and headed out into the anteroom just as Joan was arriving for work.

"Oh, Joan, I'm glad you're here," Brooke said as she struggled into her jacket. "I've signed the letters on my desk, and they can go out today. I don't know how long this parade is going to last. I'll try to call in later."

"Got a minute before you run?" Joan asked.

"Only a minute. I was supposed to be at the grand-stand about . . ." She checked her watch again. "Five minutes ago."

"This won't take long. I want you to take a look at something interesting. I found—"

"Brooke?" Devon's voice bellowed from below.

"Up here," she answered.

Devon climbed the circular stairway and stopped on the top step. He gave Joan a quick good-morning nod, then stood still for the longest moment, intently staring at Brooke. She felt her face flush all the way to her hairline as her reason for being late—not to mention sore—confronted her in one thoroughly masculine package.

He looked so handsome dressed in his gray pin-striped suit, the epitome of the successful business-man. But Brooke had another image in her mind, a softer, hazier picture of him naked and poised over her as the early light of dawn had filtered into her bed-room.

"Hi," she said softly, not completely free of the power of that lingering glow.

"Hi, yourself." Devon walked over to her, lifted her hair, and gave her an intimate kiss behind the ear. "How are you this morning?"

Brooke could have died. She didn't dare look at Joan, who she knew must be observing them as if they were aliens with purple tentacles.

"I'm fine," she said, and moved back, slightly out of his reach. "How are you?"

"Fine." He grinned. "Did you have a good night?"

"Very." As if he didn't know.

"I came to walk you over to the grandstand," he said.

"I'll meet you out front," she said, hoping he would leave and give her a chance to collect herself.

"Okay," Devon said with a half smile. "But hurry. You know how people talk when we're late."

She gave him a reprimanding shake of her head as he headed for the stairs. Devon laughed out loud, totally unbothered by her discomfort, not to mention Joan's confusion.

Brooke took a deep breath and turned to Joan. "What were you saying?"

"What was *that* all about?" Joan asked.

"Nothing."

"Didn't look like 'nothing'."

"Really, Joan. He was just being friendly. Whether I like it or not, I have to deal with him."

Joan raised her eyebrows. "Friendly? That looked more like—"

"I thought you had something to show me."

Joan bit her bottom lip, then slowly shook her head. "Forget it."

"We'll do it later, then. Okay?" Brooke asked as she hurried down the stairs.

"Yeah," Joan said. "Maybe later."

Brooke ran off with a wave, almost bumping into Devon as she exited.

"Did you have to do that?" she asked as they walked toward the end of town where the grandstand was set up.

"Do what?"

"Embarrass me in front of Joan like that."

"Embarrass you? I thought I was kissing you hello. I thought after last night I could do that without asking permission. Isn't that allowed?"

"Not in public."

"Oh," he said. "In private we can roll naked around the floor and make mad, passionate love, but in public I have to keep my distance. Is that correct? Be specific now. I don't want to *embarrass* you again."

Brooke stopped and pulled on his arm to make him face her. "If I didn't know you better, Devon Taylor, I'd say you were hurt."

"Maybe I am."

"To be hurt, one has to care."

"Who says I don't."

"You do," she said.

"Maybe I lied."

"Wouldn't be the first time."

Brooke began walking again. Devon grabbed her arm and stopped her cold. He kissed her, a long, hard kiss in broad daylight in the middle of Main Street. It was an impulsive act, indicative of his whole life. He'd thought that part was over. He thought he was in control, but that wasn't true, not true at all where Brooke was concerned.

He was fighting here, fighting for his life. The kiss deepened and with it came a mixture of emotion—hurt, anger, desire... plus something else, a strange, vulnerable feeling that wasn't completely unrecognizable. It had crept, uninvited, into his soul sometime last night. And it scared the hell out of him.

He'd been like a schoolboy this morning, sneaking out of her house at dawn, grinning in the shower as images of the night before replayed themselves in his mind. He had to stop this, had to break away from the sensuous web she was weaving around him before it was too late, before he found it impossible to walk away from her.

Devon pulled back, but Brooke's body was so limp, he had to hold her by the shoulders to stop her from crumbling onto the sidewalk. Her face had that dreamy, satisfied look, the same one she had right after they made love. A piercing stab of pleasure shot through him, leaving him shaking inside.

It's already too late, my boy, way too late.

People were stopping to stare. Devon became aware of it even if Brooke didn't. She seemed dazed. He knew the feeling. Every time he touched her, life around him faded to a dull hue. He began walking again, pulling her along with him.

"Let's get out of here. We'll have to talk about this later," he said, careful not to define "this."

"We're always *going* to talk about *this,*" Brooke said with a grin. "But whenever we do, something turns up."

Devon laughed out loud and pulled her into his arms. "You do have a way with words, Mayor Wallace." He brushed his lips against hers. "And accurate, too."

He grinned down at her. She smiled up at him. He was incorrigible. And adorable. Just looking into those bright blue eyes made her heart melt. To anyone observing, they must look like two people in love.

Her stomach took a nosedive with the thought. Well, at least one of them was. She'd stopped denying her true feelings for him somewhere around four o'clock in the morning when they'd made love on the kitchen chair.

When dawn approached, she hadn't wanted him to leave.

The thought sobered her. "We're late," she said. "They can't start the parade without us."

"Do you think they'll mind if we march sideways, like this, down Main Street?"

Brooke pulled out of his embrace, resisting the temptation to stay there all day. It felt so good, so right . . . could it really be so wrong?

"Yes," she said, "I think they'll mind."

The grandstand was set up in the front yard of an old church at the very edge of town. Chuck frantically waved them on and indicated front-row seats he'd saved for them.

The crowd was becoming restless. Devon and Brooke climbed the steps to take their places. The town council and the powers that be were already seated on the grandstand bleachers, and each was staring at Devon and her. She wondered what they were thinking about the two of them. Did they know they were lovers? Brooke gave herself a mental shake. She had to get over this instant embarrassment whenever confronted with proof of her relationship with Devon . . . and she *did* have a relationship with him. Like it or not, they were long past sneaking around. Anyway, between Joan in her office and that kiss on Main Street, Brooke figured they'd pretty much covered the entire town.

Brooke addressed the crowd that had gathered, abandoning the more formal speech she had planned to talk about the changes Lenape Bay had seen in the past year. She even managed to mention the Maiden Point project when listing the accomplishments and attractions of the town.

Her attitude toward the project was also changing, due, in no small part she was sure, to her changing attitude toward Devon. She was beginning to feel "if you can't beat them, join them." Everyone was enthusiastic about the new project, and she had to admit that there was a renewed energy around town since Devon's arrival.

Perhaps she had been overly harsh about Maiden Point because of her initial hostility toward Devon. But Chuck was right when he said Devon had changed. He had. Just looking at what he'd accomplished in the years away from Lenape Bay told of his success in the face of all the odds. After all, everyone was entitled to make mistakes in life. She'd made her share, that was for sure.

Fifteen years was a long time, and a lot could happen to alter a person's perspective on things. He was a man now, not an impetuous boy, and his maturity manifested itself in the way he walked, talked, dressed and handled himself with people. There was an air of confidence and control about him that was absent from the adolescent Devon. He was an enigma, to be sure, but could Devon really make love with her that way at night and lie to her during the day? Was he that good an actor?

It was Devon's turn to speak, and as he headed toward the podium, their gazes locked for the briefest moment. There was so much there, so many deep and powerful feelings transmitted in a split second, Brooke felt her heart skip a beat.

His speech was full of promise and optimism about the future. He renewed his commitment to the town, and with it, Brooke felt as if he were speaking directly to her. Various emotions swirled inside of her as she watched him mesmerize the crowd. A lump formed in her throat and tears filled her eyes.

She loved him. God help her, it was true.

Perhaps she had never stopped loving him. Perhaps all those years were just a cover-up, a way of living a lie and convincing herself she was satisfied with it. Brooke took a tissue out of her bag and fixed her face. This was not the time to ruminate over her choices in life—or his. If this was a new beginning, she was more than ready for it. She would welcome it with open arms.

The applause for Devon's speech was stunning. Because of the crowd's enthusiasm, the parade planners cut short the other speakers, and without further ado, the parade was on its way.

Brooke and Devon took the lead as the group lined up and headed toward the center of town. They fell into step behind the school's marching band and waved to the bystanders. Devon looked as if he were having a high old time, and Brooke commented on it. He didn't deny it, and she took the opportunity to congratulate him on his speech.

"Ever think about going into politics?" she asked.

"Worried about your job?"

"I might have to. If you stay in town."

"Still not convinced I'm staying?"

Brooke hesitated, then slowly shook her head.

Devon leaned toward her, his mouth near her ear. "If last night didn't prove anything—"

"Devon..." she warned.

He laughed. "Okay. No more embarrassing moments in public, Mayor Wallace."

Devon did take her hand, though, and she didn't argue with that, choosing to ignore the curious glances that came their way. When the parade reached its end, the crowd dispersed. Brooke and Devon lingered, browsing at the street vendors' fare along the way.

"Devon! Over here." Mrs. Antonelli waved them toward the bakery's open-air stand. "Have a taste." The grandmotherly woman leaned forward and stuffed a miniature chocolate éclair into his mouth. She turned to Brooke. "He loved these when he was a little boy." She shook her finger in Devon's face. "Used to steal them, too!"

Devon laughed with his mouth full, grabbing Mrs. Antonelli's wagging finger in his fist. "You were crazy about me, Mrs. Antonelli."

"Go on, go on," she said with a smile and a shake of her head. "Watch him," she said to Brooke. "He's a devil, that one."

"Don't I know it," Brooke answered.

Devon and Brooke continued walking. "I'd forgotten all about that," he said. "It's true, though. I did sneak in and steal those éclairs. Mrs. Antonelli would come screaming and chasing me out the door. But she never caught me."

"Naturally," Brooke said.

Devon grinned. "I was a real hell-raiser, wasn't I?"

"You still are."

"You weren't complaining last night."

"Last night was . . . different."

"Why?"

"Because you took me by surprise."

"You didn't expect me?" he asked.

"No, Devon. I didn't expect you. You broke into my house. Or did you forget that little fact?"

"I can't believe you didn't expect me to come to you. There you were lying on the couch, naked, soft music in the background, a fire going. Looked to me like you were just waiting for me to show up."

She shook her head. "You're impossible."

Devon laughed, and pulled her to him. He was doing a lot of that lately: laughing and holding Brooke. Granted, everything was going according to plan, so much so that at times it worried him. But these feelings he was having for her were something he hadn't planned on. This new, budding relationship was one of those "intangibles" he had thought he'd be prepared for. He wasn't. He wouldn't deny that seducing her had crossed his mind. What he hadn't counted on was being seduced himself.

Trouble was, he was having a good time, a damned good time. In fact, he couldn't remember ever being happier than he was right now, walking down the main street of this sleepy little bay town he used to call home with his childhood sweetheart on his arm.

What could be simpler?

What could be better?

What could be more dangerous?

Last night had been a turning point. He'd made light of it with Brooke, but that was more for his sake than hers. The fact was he hadn't wanted the night to end, hadn't wanted to leave her this morning. If he could have, he would have whisked her away to an isolated island where no one knew them, where they could eat, drink, sleep, and make love without any outside interference from anyone . . . including himself.

The time was fast approaching when his "consortium" would have to come up with closing money on the model unit. Since there was no consortium, there would be no payment, and the bank would get stuck with the subsequent tab. That suited him just fine, as the fulfillment of all his dreams was close at hand.

What didn't suit him as fine was the effect all of this was going to have on Brooke. She was beginning to feel things for him again. Even though the words weren't there, her body language last night spoke volumes. He should be feeling a deep sense of satisfaction over the fact that she was falling in love with him again, but there seemed to be a doubled-edged sword here. The feeling was *not* supposed to be mutual.

It was. If the time at his house, in Chaz's bed had been a "ten," last night had to rate somewhere off the chart. For that all too short time, he had lost himself in her. There was no Devon Taylor last night. He'd ceased to exist. They'd reached for something, and together they'd found it. It was profound, and so complete, he couldn't remember ever feeling that alive, that needed, that wanted.

Yes, he could. Once before. Long ago in a dilapidated cabin on the beach on a moonless June night.

He had called it love then; he didn't dare call it that now. Whatever the case, his taste for revenge—as far as Brooke was concerned—was fading fast, leaving in its place the warm afterglow of...what? Emotions he hadn't had to deal with in a very long time were bubbling close to the surface.

He realized that with all the planning he'd done regarding his return to Lenape Bay, he hadn't given any thought at all to what he would do after he'd exacted his revenge. The future was one big question mark. He had no idea what he was going to do with Brooke or these feelings she'd regenerated, and it scared the holy hell out of him.

Be that as it may, he was still committed to his original course of action. It was too late to turn back now even if he wanted to—which, he kept reminding himself, he didn't.

"Devon, Brooke! Wait up!" They turned in time to see Chuck jog across the street. "I wanted to talk to you."

"How's it going?" Devon asked.

"Good. Real good. Have you been out to the site?"

"Not in a couple of days," Devon said.

"Well, I was there early this morning, and you won't believe how much work they've done! Looks like we'll be ready to close soon," Chuck said.

"Possibly within weeks," Devon said.

"Really?" Brooke interjected.

"Yep."

"That's great!" Chuck said. "Shall we pick a date for the closing?"

Devon smiled. "Sure, Chuck. Be my guest."

"When is good for you?" Chuck asked.

"I'll let you choose," Devon said.

"Okay. I'll get the ball rolling and have the papers drawn up." He looked at Brooke. "Isn't this exciting?"

"Yes," she agreed. "It is."

And she meant it. Once Devon closed on the first unit, there would be no reason to doubt him anymore. He would be as committed to the project as the bank.

She looked up at Devon. "It all seems to have happened so fast," she said after Chuck took his leave.

"It all depends on how you look at it," Devon said.

Brooke gave him a puzzled look. Wrapping an arm around her shoulders, he hugged her to him. "Come on, let's get some lunch. That éclair was just a tease. I need some real food.''

They entered Wylie's Luncheonette. The place was crowded with patrons, and they had to wait for a booth. Townspeople who passed by remarked on their respective speeches, and some tried to outdo each other with anecdotes about Devon's escapades from the past.

Brooke watched Devon as he joked and traded stories with some of the old-timers. He seemed relaxed, at ease, and perfectly at home here...even more so than when he'd actually lived here. That warmed her more than anything. When he reached out and took hold of her hand, she admitted that he had won her over.

She believed him.

Both frightened and excited, Brooke could do nothing to stop the glimmer of hope for a future with him from peeking over the horizon of her heart.

''I'd forgotten half of those stories,'' Devon said as they slid into a booth near the back of the luncheonette.

''No one else has. It seems everyone has a favorite 'Devon story' to tell.''

Devon grinned and waved to a group who was leaving. ''They're good people,'' he said.

''You sound surprised by that.''

''I suppose I am,'' he said. ''I don't have very many fond memories of Lenape Bay. But I guess I *chose* not to remember some of the good times.''

''Sometimes it's better to put the past behind you,'' she said softly.

Devon looked into her eyes. He knew exactly what Brooke was leading up to. She wanted to talk...about them, but he wasn't prepared to pour his heart out to her. Not yet. Maybe not ever. There'd be time enough to deal with all of this after the closing, after he'd fulfilled his plan.

He wondered how she would feel about him then. If he explained his reasons to her, would she even try to understand? He doubted it. And because of that, he had to keep his eye on the prize, not on the dreamy look on Brooke's face. Last night was last night, but tomorrow...well tomorrow was another day, as the saying went, and every tomorrow brought them one day closer to the day of reckoning.

"Let's order," he said, and lifted the oversize menu in front of his face.

Brooke allowed him to avoid the conversation and picked up her own menu. He was uncomfortable talking about his feelings. That was fine. For now. In fact, his discomfort only proved one thing to her: he was feeling too much, more that he could handle. That was fine, too. She could wait a little bit longer. She'd waited fifteen years.

After lunch, they walked the rest of the way to her office arm-in-arm. Townspeople and shopkeepers grinned and waved as they passed, but it didn't matter to Brooke what anyone thought anymore. At the entrance to her building, Devon stopped.

"I'm going to take a ride over to the site. Let's go out of town for dinner tonight. Just the two of us."

"Okay," she said.

"Why don't you stop by the house around seven. I've done some work upstairs that I'd like to show off. We can leave after that."

"Sounds fine," she said as she gazed up into his eyes.

Devon tilted her chin up and studied her dreamy expression. His body reacted to it like a match to a flame. Mindful of where they were, he pulled her into the deserted vestibule of the office building. Tucking her into him, he pushed her up against the wall. With hips pressed intimately to her, he bent his head and brushed his mouth against her lips. She responded by wrapping her arms around his neck and fitting herself into his body. As far as he was concerned, tonight couldn't come soon enough. Apparently she felt the same way.

A noise from upstairs alerted them to unwelcome company. Devon backed away from her. He held the front door open and looked at her over his shoulder. Brooke was standing still, resting against the wall, waiting for... him.

He pointed to her as he left. "Oh, babe," he said softly, "Hold that thought."

Ten

***

Brooke watched him walk away, then swung around and slowly climbed the stairs to her office. Sometimes she wished she was a little less conscientious, the type of person who would just take off. She was in the mood to play hooky. She grinned to herself. In bed.

Joan was typing efficiently as Brooke hit the top step. She took a deep breath and blew it out. Time to get back to business.

"How'd it go?" Joan asked.

"The parade? Fine."

Joan nodded toward the clock on the wall. "Lasted longer than I thought."

"Devon and I had lunch afterward, then walked around. Any messages?" she asked.

"Just a few. Nothing urgent."

"Good. I'm in no mood for 'urgent.' My feet are killing me."

Brooke flopped into her chair and took off her shoes.
"Brooke?"

She glanced at Joan in the doorway. "Yes?"

"Got a minute to look at something?"

"Oh, sure. Come on in. Is this what you wanted to go
over earlier?" Brooke said as she massaged the sole of
her foot.

Joan bit her lip, then nodded. "Yes. Some letters.
From the Maiden Point file."

Brooke's head snapped up. "What letters?"

Joan laid them out on the desk. "These."

Brooke studied them. They were letters of intent from
various companies in Devon's consortium. All were
typed on neat letterhead and seemed direct and to the
point.

"What am I looking for?"

"Here." Joan pointed to the bottom of each letter.
"Do you see anything odd about the signatures?"

"No."

"Look closer. See how the letter 'i' is dotted?"

"Yes, with little circles instead of dots."

"Well," Joan said, "they're all the same." She
pointed to four of the letters. "Anywhere there is an 'i'
in the signatures, it's dotted with a circle. And each of
these letters is from a different company."

Brooke felt her stomach clench. "Then the same
person signed each letter."

"Looks that way."

Brooke picked up two letters and compared them.
One was from a company in southern California, another from Arizona. "How could two companies so far
away from each other have the same person signing letters?"

"Maybe they aren't that far away from each other."

Brooke stared at Joan as the reality of her words seeped into her brain. Her insides took an elevator nosedive, and her hand began to shake. "Leave these with me."

"But—"

"No, Joan. This is something I have to do myself. Thank you for all your help on this, but, please, just go home now. It's late anyway."

"I can help—"

"Please, Joan. No. Just shut the door."

Joan did as requested, but reluctantly. When the door closed, Brooke wrapped her arms around her middle and held herself together. She had to. She was nauseous with fright and fear. All the good feelings from earlier in the day vanished in an instant. All the doubts and mistrust resurfaced with the force of an erupting volcano.

This couldn't be what it appeared to be, she rationalized. There had to be some explanation. Not after all that had happened. Not after all he'd said. Not after last night. He couldn't . . .

Brooke didn't know how long she'd stared into space going over and over everything he'd said, but when she looked up, it was dark, and all was quiet save for a light rain tapping against the window.

She had to find out what this meant. Straightening her chair, she reviewed the letters again. There was no doubt about it. The same person signed all four letters. Letters from different companies miles apart from each other. It wasn't something easily spotted. She could understand how Chuck's people would never have noticed such a thing, especially if more than one person was working on the project, which was the case with Maiden Point.

Her hand shook as she held the first letter. She copied down the telephone number from the upper right-hand corner of the paper, then repeated the same for the others. Comparing them, she discovered that two of the four had the same number with different extensions. One was a straight 800 number, and the other, a personalized call-letter number that, when translated, was the same as the toll-free one.

It was clear that all these companies were related in some way. But what way? And how did that relationship affect Maiden Point? She dialed the toll-free number. A woman answered and identified the company. Brooke politely excused herself. A minute later she tried the call-letter number's extension. When the same woman answered, identifying a different company, a heartsick Brooke muttered some incoherent explanation and hung up.

Her entire body was shaking by this time. Reaching into herself for a reserve of strength she wasn't sure she possessed, Brooke flipped through her address file. She pulled out Devon's business card for his California office. For the longest time she just stared at it before dialing the number.

"Taylor Properties. May I help you? Hello? Is anyone there?"

The voice was the same.

Slowly, Brooke cradled the phone. She rose and walked blindly to the ladies' room. Turning the tap on full blast, she ran cold water across her wrists. She felt faint. Supporting herself on the sides of the sink, she bent her head and breathed deeply to clear the light-headedness.

There was only one thing to do. She had to confront him. Had to hear every gory detail of this obvious trap from his own lips, those very same lips that . . .

Let him tell her to her face how he'd lied to her, how he'd lied to all of them. Let him deny it.

Brooke looked up into the mirror. The dreamy look was gone, in its place was despair and strained determination. She turned off the water and dried her hands.

"I told you so," she said aloud to her reflection.

She had been right about him all along. She could go to Chuck and flaunt it in his face. She could tell the whole town and vindicate herself. But she wouldn't. The thought made her sick. Besides, she needed more proof. There had to be something concrete to show the council that would make them sit up and take notice, to make them not think she was crying wolf again.

His office!

Just below her were his desk and file cabinet. If he was fronting for four different companies, there had to be something down there that would corroborate her findings.

Brooke left the ladies' room and headed for the stairs. She tested the knob to his office door. Locked. Of course, she thought, he wouldn't want anyone prowling around poking their noses into his business, now would he?

After a quick trip back upstairs for her handbag, Brooke returned with a hairpin. She inserted it into the lock and wiggled it around.

"Two can play the same game, Devon Taylor," she said aloud, then chided herself. She needed no justification for what she was doing.

Much to her surprise, the lock clicked and the knob turned easily in her hand. With a quick glance over her shoulder, Brooke slipped inside.

Devon parked the car at the curb. Main Street was all but deserted, as the weather had taken a bad turn, cutting short any evening Octoberfest plans. It was cold and wet, the kind of deep-bone damp that is unique to the shore area. He turned off the engine and sat quietly for a long moment. A fine mist soon covered the windshield.

Perhaps the weather was contributing to his melancholy mood. Though he'd never been one to dabble in the paranormal, something had come over him as he'd prepared for his evening with Brooke. The feeling was indescribable, a sort of premonition that all was not as it appeared to be. It had become so strong, so urgent, that he had to act on it.

It hadn't surprised him to find Brooke's cottage empty. Somehow he'd known that whatever was going on, it had nothing to do with what was between them, but rather *around* them. He'd followed his instincts to town. Her car was the only one left in the parking lot. Why was she still here when she was supposed to meet him at his house a half hour ago?

He slid out of the Jaguar and stood on the sidewalk, jiggling his keys in his hand, trying to decide on the best course of action. He entered the building. The hallway light was off, and he flipped the switch. He was just about to climb onto the first step when he was distracted by the sound of a file cabinet being slammed shut. He turned in the direction of the sound. It was coming from his office.

Devon's insides tightened. He walked toward the door, picking through his key ring for the correct key to insert into the lock. He needn't have bothered. The door was open. He checked the knob. A few scratches, but no permanent damage. All in all, a pretty neat job.

As Devon hit the overhead light switch, he was greeted by Brooke's gasp of surprise. "You pick a pretty mean lock, Mayor Wallace," he said.

Brooke was caught, and her pulse began to hammer in her head. She lifted her chin in defiance. She wouldn't show her fear. Not to him. Never to him.

"I'll take that as a compliment. From you."

"Why break in, Brooke? If there was something you wanted, all you had to do was ask."

"I didn't think you'd want to show me these particular files," she said.

"What files are they?"

"Files on your consortium."

"Oh. I see," he said as he walked toward her. He stopped a few feet from the desk. "And have you found what you were looking for?"

"I'm not sure."

"What *are* you looking for?"

"Proof. To bury you, Devon."

He laughed, flipped the key ring and slipped it back into his jacket pocket. "So dramatic, Brooke. How can I help?" he asked.

Smooth as ice, Brooke thought, so smooth, you could skate on him. "I don't know, Devon."

"If you'll tell me what you're specifically looking for, maybe I can."

Brooke held up a paper. Devon walked toward her and took it from her hand. He read over the list of his so-called consortium. A derisive half smile creased his face. So she knew. How, he wasn't yet sure. It didn't really matter anyway. He looked at her. Her face was implacable. Hard. Not a trace of a dream present. The tightening in his gut became an outright ache. Many times over the past several days he'd wondered how she'd react when she found out.

Now he knew.

"What do you want to know?" he asked and handed the paper back to her.

"These companies who are investing in Maiden Point. Who do they belong to?"

Devon pulled out a chair and sat. If she intended to play cat and mouse with him, he might as well get comfortable.

He blew out a breath. "Why don't you tell me, babe. You seem to have it all figured out. Who do you think they belong to?"

"From what I can tell, at least four of the ten belong to you. Bogus companies, am I right?"

He nodded. "Yes."

Brooke felt her throat close. She'd thought he'd deny it, thought he'd at least attempt to convince her of his innocence. His admission of guilt all but took the wind out of her sails.

"You admit it? You admit that these companies are just fronts for Taylor Properties?"

"I already said yes, Brooke. What more do you want from me?"

"What I've always wanted from you, Devon. Answers to my questions. The truth."

"Fire away."

He was so nonchalant, so unbothered. It seemed to Brooke as if he had been waiting—no, planning—a meeting such as this from the very beginning. Perhaps he had. Perhaps this was all part of his elaborate scheme to take down the Pattersens and the town in one fell swoop. She took a deep breath. Whatever the case, she had to play the game, even if it was his game, even if he was the one with all the cards and all the rules on his side.

"How many of the companies in the consortium are yours?"

"All of them."

"All . . . ?" Brooke's hands began to shake. She put the paper down on the desk and grabbed onto the edge. "What about the closing?"

"What about it?"

"Are you going to come up with the money?"

"No."

"No? Just no? No explanation. You're just going to let the bank take the fall? Just like that?"

"Just like that."

"And how do you think you'll get away with it, Devon? It's not like we don't know where you live."

"I can be out of here in ten minutes, Brooke. Five, if I have to."

"I don't believe this."

Devon stood. "What don't you believe, Brooke?"

"I don't believe you're not denying it."

"Is that what you want me to do? I can, you know." He stood and rested both hands on the desk. His face was an inch from hers. He reached up and caressed her face with the tips of his fingers. "I can deny it all. And you'd believe me, Brooke. You know you would."

Brooke felt a shudder run through her body. Still, even now, his touch was electric, and she leaned into it. She couldn't help but respond; she was as conditioned as Pavlov's dog.

She looked into his mesmerizing blue eyes and knew he was right. He could convince her that she was mistaken. He could talk her out of believing what she was seeing with her own eyes. And she *would* believe him. It would be so easy, it was pathetic.

Brooke pulled away, a deliberate, painful move. "You know I'm going straight to Chuck with this information."

Devon shrugged. "Go right ahead. There's nothing to be done about it now. The closing is set. The work has been done. The contractors want to be paid. They're funny that way."

Brooke folded her hands in front of her, resting them on top of the desk. She was sick to her stomach, and afraid she would embarrass herself. Reaching as deep down into herself as she was able, she fought against the gamut of emotions running through her brain and, at the same time, tried to keep her face neutral. She knew Devon well enough to know that a tantrum would not work with him. She opted for controlled calm.

"Why, Devon? Will you tell me that at least?"

"You're so smart, Brooke. You figured all this out—" he said with a wave of his hand "—haven't you figured that out yet? I would have thought my motives would have been clear to you most of all."

"You seem to have this 'thing' against my family," she began. "You hate us, and I never did understand why. My father didn't like you when we dated, I'll grant you that, but he did try to help your family. I know that for a fact," she said.

"Oh, he helped us all right. Helped us by bankrupting my father's business. Helped us by mortgaging my mother's home, then using it to run me out of town."

Her stomach twisted. "That's not true," she said. "My father was an honest man."

"Your father was a bastard."

"Devon, don't you dare—"

"Oh, babe, I do dare. I dare plenty. My only regret is that your darling father is not alive to see this happening to his precious bank."

"You can't do this, Devon."

"It's already done."

"What about Chuck?"

"Chuck is in over his head. Always was. When he was Daddy's errand boy, it was easy. But now he's on his own. It's payback time."

"Chuck never hurt you. Your victory is empty, Devon. Chuck is not my father."

Devon stared at her long and hard. "He'll have to do."

"What about the townspeople? The Antonellis and the others, the ones you called 'good people'? They'll be devastated by this."

"Sometimes innocent people get hurt," he said.

"Like you? Like your mother?" When Devon didn't respond, she continued. "I'm sorry for what my father did to you, Devon. If I could change the past, I would, but I can't. All I can try to do is stop you from making the same mistake he did."

"It's too late for changes, Brooke."

"It's never too late. Not if you want to. I'll help you. I'll—"

"Did you ever think that maybe I don't want your help? That I don't *want* to change anything. That this is exactly what I do want?"

She swallowed the tears that threatened to choke her. "Then I feel sorry for you," she said softly.

Devon made a derisive sound. "It all comes back to *me* again, doesn't it? Never you, never your family. Only me. All Devon's fault. Always was, always will be. Well, it's not about *me*, babe. It's about justice."

"That's why you came back? For some warped sense of justice?"

Devon stared at her for the longest moment. He could not believe that this display of naiveté was genuine. She drove him crazy with this on-again, off-again fragility that made absolutely no sense to him. He muttered an expletive, then abruptly swung away from her.

Brooke watched as he ran a hand through his hair. He was upset, and that suited her just fine. No matter what he felt about her, or her family for that matter, she had to find a way to get through to him, not just for Chuck and the bank, but for the town, as well.

She wouldn't begin to think about where she fit in to all this.

His back was to her. When he spoke, his voice was so low, she had to strain to hear him. "Did you really think I'd never come back?" He turned slowly. "Didn't you understand me at all? Didn't you realize that someday you would have to pay for what you did?"

"Devon, what are you talking about? What did we do?"

"What did you do? Come on, Brooke, let's not re-hash the whole thing."

She walked over to him and placed a hand on his arm. "Please, Devon. Tell me what you're talking about."

Devon stared at her hand on his arm. He didn't want to do this, didn't want to discuss the past, especially not with her. He looked at the delicate, warm hand on his arm, and shut his eyes. But he couldn't shut out the way his body responded to her nearness, to her touch. He shook his head, and gave up the fight.

"I'm talking about you, your brother, and most of all, your father, and what he did to me and my family. Or have you just forgotten all that?"

"I haven't forgotten anything. You're the one who seems to have forgotten how you left, and why. If anyone needs to apologize, it's you, not me, or my family."

Devon stared at her incredulously. "And that's how you see it?"

"Yes, that's how it was."

His stomach a maze of knots, Devon reached up and held her at arm's length, his crystal-blue eyes fixing her with a penetrating gaze. He never thought she could hurt him again, not after all these years. He'd thought he was immune.

"God, you're a cool one. I guess I never could reconcile myself to how cool you really are. But I should have known better. I've got the same feeling right now that I had when I saw you standing at your window that morning. I waited for you to come running to me, did you know that? Even as Chuck mocked me, threatened me with the cops, I still waited. Like a fool. And you, cool as could be, just shut the curtains and walked away." His hands tightened on her arms, and he gave her a shake. "I can still feel the heat of the sun burning my neck as I sat there waiting for you. I can still smell the dust from the road. It was one of those moments in life that you never forget." He released her, and she fell back against the desk. "At least it was for me."

Brooke grabbed his arm before he could move away. Her heart was pounding. "What do you mean? When did you come to the house?"

"The morning after the prom. You never showed up at the cabin. Chaz did. He said you weren't coming. I didn't believe him. I went after you."

"That's crazy. My father didn't know about the cabin."

"Oh, no? Then who was that with a baseball bat ready to bash my skull in for having sex with his 'underage' daughter? He said you'd told him where to find me."

"Devon, I never told my father where you were. After he left for the bank, I packed a bag and walked through the dunes to meet you at the cabin. When I got there, you were gone. I never heard from you again."

Devon's heart began to beat double time in his chest. Why was she doing this? Why was she saying this after all this time? "Don't lie to me, Brooke. What's the point?"

Brooke felt frightened, and she wasn't sure why. Something was terribly wrong here. What had her father done? Had he lied to both of them? Had he manipulated them into betraying each other? She didn't know what had happened that day fifteen years ago. All she did know was that she had to convince him that she had nothing to do with it.

"I'm not lying. How could you believe I would do that? I loved you then, Devon." She threw her arms around him, and hugged him to her. "God help me. I love you now."

It took her a moment to realize that Devon was not holding her. His arms were at his sides, his body stiff and unrelenting. She let go and took a step back from him.

When he spoke, his voice was soft, almost deathly so. "I *saw* you at the window, Brooke. I *saw* the curtains shut. I'm not crazy, and I'm not stupid. Don't try to whitewash the truth.''

He didn't believe her. But then, why should he? If all he said was true, why should he believe anything any Pattersen told him? The track record of lies was too strong to be denied. Her entire body throbbed with sorrow and fear—sorrow for the past, and fear for the future. She needed to find a way to reach him, to make him believe her.

Brooke stroked his face. "I'm not. Oh, Devon, please believe me. I'm telling the truth, I swear to you.''

Devon grabbed her upper arms with all intentions of pushing her away from him. He didn't know what she was up to, and he didn't care to know. If this was another one of her tricks, he wasn't about to fall for it at this late date.

But when she lifted her face to him, the sight of her tear-filled eyes ripped his already battered heart to shreds. Devon didn't think of the consequences. He slanted his mouth across hers and kissed her. It was a joyless kiss, filled with frustration, laced with passion, tinged with remorse.

Brooke's tongue mated with his as she kissed him back with her entire being. It was as if she instinctively knew that this may be the last time they ever kissed. She felt as if she were clawing her way up the side of a steep mountain, her footing unsure, the road crumbling beneath her. She clung to the kiss as if it were the only solid thing of substance to hang on to, her salvation. In a way, it was just that.

It was her last chance to reach him.

Devon broke the kiss, but she refused to be pushed away. She reached up and pulled his head back down to hers. Devon kissed her again, covering her mouth with his own in an almost savage attempt to devour her. She gave as good as she got, taking advantage of his capitulation.

Boldly she ran her hands over him. She unbuttoned his shirt and caressed his chest, and lower. His sex was straining against the fabric of his pants, and she stroked him intimately. She undid his pants and slipped her hand inside. He was hot, swollen and rock-hard.

"Brooke..."

"You love me, Devon, you know you do. You couldn't feel like this if you didn't."

"That's not love, babe," he said as he grabbed her wrist. "That's lust."

Brooke looked up at him, ignoring the arrow of hurt that stung her heart. "Prove it."

Devon's eyes darkened with the challenge. He spun her around and lifted her onto the desk. In less than a minute, her undergarments were in a heap on the floor and he was between her legs. He lifted her skirt and in one powerful thrust, joined them.

Brooke rejoiced in his urgency. She arched her back to accept him more fully. She looped her arms around his neck, wrapped her legs around his waist, and pulled him onto the desk on top of her.

The file folders scattered across the desk and flew haphazardly to the floor around them. They were oblivious to all around them except the beat of their hearts and the rhythm of their bodies. They made love in a frenzy, as if they were the two last people on earth and this was the very last time they would ever be together.

Then, just as suddenly, it gentled. Devon's lips rained tiny nibbling kisses on her cheeks, eyes and the special soft spot behind her ear. He kissed her neck, and nudged aside the material of her blouse to rub his mouth against her breasts. When he looked up at Brooke, her eyes were misty, and a thin line of tears streamed from their corners into her hairline. He wiped the wetness away with the pads of his thumbs.

"I love you," she whispered, determined that he know it, even if he refused to believe it.

Devon shut his eyes, attempting if not succeeding to shut his heart to her words and the effect they were having on his body. His throat was swollen with pain, confusion and desire. He couldn't speak, so he answered her in the only way he knew how. With the power of his body.

He made love to her with a tenderness that had been nestled deep in the recesses of his soul. It had been hidden there so long, he'd forgotten it, forgotten the feeling of giving so freely, so lovingly that he lost all sense of time, reason . . . himself.

Devon held her to him as he pushed off the desk and stood. Brooke balanced at the edge of the desk. He filled her. She shut her eyes and danced with him to an erotic inner music, a slow, sensuous song all their own. As her body began its ascent, Brooke began to tremble, and gripped his shoulders for support. Soon she was out of control, her body bucking into his, striving to get closer, closer, as she tightened her grip on him. Tiny whimpers of pleasure stole up from her throat, and the sounds were muffled into his neck.

The sounds drove him crazy, close to the brink of his own climax. Devon felt her tighten around him in spasms of joyful release. She nuzzled his neck and sought his mouth with a fervor that allowed no dissent. He met her halfway, covering her open mouth with his own, kissing her with emotions fifteen years in the making. He cried out her name, and let himself go, gifting her with everything he possessed—his heart, his soul, his very essence.

When it was over, he didn't move; he couldn't. Past memories and present feelings were swirling together in a whirlpool in his head. He needed time. He had to think, get out of here, get away from her. Better yet, away from the town. The thought of going home left him cold. Chaz's house was the last place he wanted to be.

He looked at Brooke. She was studying his face, waiting for him to say something—anything—to reassure her that he had changed his mind. He caressed her face with his fingertips, bent his head and kissed her gently on the lips.

She was right about one thing. He did love her. But believing her was something else. He wasn't ready for that; maybe he never would be.

Devon turned from her. He picked up her clothing.

"This shouldn't have happened," he said as he held out her undergarments.

"Why, Devon? It's what always happens when we're alone together. We love each other. Why should tonight be so different?"

"Whether we love each other or not isn't the point. The charade is over, Brooke."

Her heart leaped in her chest. He didn't deny it. "There was never a charade, Devon. If what you say is true, we were both fooled by my father."

Devon shook his head, still unable to accept what she was saying. "Conveniently for you, Chaz is dead. He can't answer any questions."

"But Chuck isn't," she said. "I wasn't at the house that morning, Devon. I was on my way to meet you."

For the longest time, he stared at her. He shook his head as if to clear it, as if to reassure himself that they were having the same conversation about the same day in their lives. As much as he wanted—needed—to believe her, old habits died hard. If what she said was true, it would alter everything he'd believed to be so for the past fifteen years. It would change all the rules. He wouldn't know what to do if those rules changed at this point in time. His world would be thrown into a tailspin... and his heart along with it.

But...could it be true? Could it be that she'd *wanted* to go away with him? Could it be so simple that they just got their wires crossed that day, that they let their own insecurities and other people's lies keep them apart all these years?

No. He couldn't accept that. He wouldn't. Without a word he walked toward the door and opened it. Before he left, he turned. "If it wasn't you at the window that morning, Brooke, then who was it?"

"I don't know," she said.

But I'm going to find out.

Eleven

Her brother's house was completely dark and closed tight for the night when Brooke arrived. She rang the bell once, twice, and when no one answered, she pounded on the door. A light switched on in the hallway at the same time the door swung open.

"What...? Brooke?"

"Let me in, Chuck. I have to talk to you."

"At this hour? Do you know what time it is?"

"No, I don't know what time it is, and I don't care."

"Can't this wait until tomorrow?"

"No, it can't," she said, and pushed past him, stomping through his living room and into the kitchen.

"Can't you be quiet?" Chuck said in a harsh whisper as he followed behind her. "Lotty's sleeping."

Brooke turned to him. Her face was hard, tense, angry.

"What is it?" Chuck said. "Did somebody die?"

"Not yet."

"What—"

"Make some coffee, Chuck. This is going to be a long night."

"Brooke, I can't stay up all night talking. I have an important meeting at the bank tomorrow morning at eight."

"I wouldn't worry so much about the bank if I were you, Chuck. In another month, there may not *be* a bank at all."

Chuck's expression sobered. "What do you mean?"

"Maiden Point."

Chuck grimaced. "Oh, you're not going to start that old stuff again."

"No, no old stuff. New stuff. I've just left Devon."

"And . . . ? Did he say anything about the closing?"

"No, not much," she said. "Only that there isn't going to be one."

Chuck blanched. "Brooke, what the hell is going on? What are you talking about?"

"I'm talking about lies, Chuck. Deep down, hidden lies. Lies which are so embedded in your being that after a while, they become the truth."

"What lies?" Chuck asked warily.

She plunked her handbag onto the tabletop and put a hand on her hip. "Tell me about the morning after my senior prom, Chuck."

Chuck turned from her. He walked over to the stove and filled the pot with water, then flipped on the gas jet. He picked two cups off the mug rack and filled them with heaping teaspoons of instant coffee. "What about it?"

"What really happened that morning?"

"Devon left town."

"I know that, Chuck. Tell me something I don't know."

"Are we talking about Daddy and Devon?"

Brooke felt her stomach drop. "Yes. What happened with Daddy and Devon, Chuck? I want to know the truth."

Chuck blew out a breath. "All right. I should have told you years ago. I even tried to talk about it a time or two, but you always cut me off, so I figured you really didn't want to know. I thought it best to let sleeping dogs lie."

"Tell me now."

The pot whistled, and Chuck lifted it off the stove. He stirred with one hand as he filled each mug. "Daddy and I went out to the cabin early that morning. Daddy was furious about the Caddy and the bank window. I'd never seen him so out of control. I tell you, I thought he was going to kill Devon. When he took my baseball bat out of the garage, I was sure of it."

"How did Daddy know about the cabin? I never told him. I never told anyone."

"I knew about it. I'd followed you there a couple of times when you'd sneaked out to meet Devon. I figured that's where he'd be that morning."

"What did Daddy do to Devon?"

"Well, he didn't beat him up, if that's what you mean. He could have. And he would have gotten away with it. It was plain to see that the two of you had spent the night together. Daddy would have only been taking care of his own if he had."

"But Daddy wasn't like that, was he, Chuck? Daddy had other ways of dealing with people he didn't like. What did he say to Devon?"

"He told him to get out of town."

"Or..."

"Or he'd press charges about the bank. About you, too."

"And that's all?" she asked.

"As far as I can remember."

"That wouldn't have scared Devon off, Chuck. You know how he'd react to something like that. It would have made him more determined than ever to stay, if only to defy Daddy. There had to be something else. Something more."

Chuck's face brightened as if a light bulb just went on above it. "His mother's house! That was it. I'd forgotten about that. Daddy told him he'd foreclose on the house and throw his mother out in the street. That's what did it."

Brooke shut her eyes tight. The sick feeling from earlier in the day returned, only worse this time. Devon was right. He had been twisted and turned and put through a wringer by her father...and she had never been even remotely aware of it.

"He called Daddy a bastard," she said with a mirthless laugh. "I defended him. I said he was an honest man."

"Daddy was both. The trouble was that he and Devon were too much alike. Lenape Bay wasn't big enough for both of them. Devon was too young to fight someone like Chaz Pattersen. It was a lost cause from the very beginning. Devon just wouldn't face it. Not until he was forced to."

"And we played right into Daddy's hands. Both of us."

"What choice did we have, Brooke? You knew how Daddy was. He had to control everything. Us. The town. Everything."

"We could have said no."

Chuck shook his head. "And where would that have gotten us? We were kids. He was not only our father, he was our god. I'm still trying to slip out from under his shadow."

"Chuck—"

"No, don't try to placate me. You've been doing that for years. I know what you're thinking. You were against Maiden Point from the very beginning. I fell for Devon's line just like I fell for Daddy's."

"I'm here to find out the truth, Chuck, not point fingers. Lord knows if I do that I'll have to start with myself. I've lived the better part of my life believing a pack of lies."

Why hadn't she ever questioned her father directly? Was it because she hadn't wanted to scrutinize the father she adored too closely? Was that the reason? Or was it that she was afraid of what she would hear?

It had been easier to blame it all on Devon, easier to believe he could make love to her and then leave her cold. Devon was the wild one. Devon was the devil in disguise. Devon was the one who stole her heart, her soul, and left her shattered. Why had she never thought about Devon's motives, Devon's feelings, Devon's reasons?

She shook her head. It was too late for tears, too late for recriminations. She'd given up those rights years ago when she'd taken the easy way out.

Brooke sipped her coffee and looked over the rim at her brother. Chuck cradled his head in his hands and returned her stare.

"Where does all this leave us, Brooke? Is he really going to default on the loans?"

"So he says."

"We'll all go down hard if he does."

"I know."

Chuck stood and walked over to the sink. He poured the remaining coffee down the drain. "You know something? I never really hated Devon. Never. Not even when he used to beat me up all the time when we were kids. I always respected him. Sometimes I even wished I could be like him. It's funny. There were only two men in my life that I felt that way about." He gave her a sad grin. "Devon . . . and Daddy."

Brooke stood and wrapped her arms around her brother.

"What are we going to do, Brooke?"

"Try to change his mind."

Chuck pulled back from her. "How?"

"Maybe with the truth? I don't know. I haven't figured that out yet. The first thing to do is talk to him."

Brooke picked up her purse. She followed her brother to the front door. It was dawn, and the sky was beginning to lighten. She gave her brother a peck on the cheek, and turned to leave.

"Call me," he said.

She nodded and turned toward the door. "Oh," she said. "One more thing. Devon mentioned coming to our house that morning looking for me. He said he saw me in the upstairs window. Who was that, Chuck? Who was upstairs pretending to be me?"

"It was Lotty."

"Lotty!"

Chuck smirked. "You weren't the only one fooling around behind Daddy's back. We'd been in my room but when I heard Devon's motorcycle, I came out to see what he wanted. Lotty ran to your room to watch."

"I don't believe it . . . Lotty!"

"Did I hear my name?"

Brooke looked at the stairway. Halfway up stood her sister-in-law dressed in a puff-pink bathrobe and matching slippers. She had a neat hairnet tied around her head.

Chuck turned to his wife and held out his arm. "I was just telling Brooke about how you and I used to sneak into my house on the bay for a little hanky-panky."

"Oh, Chuck, go on..." Lotty said with the wave of her hand. "Why would you be telling your sister about that now?" She turned to Brooke. "Don't you go listening to any of his tales, Brooke. That was a long time ago. We were kids... only kids. We're different people now."

Brooke grinned at the absurdity of it all. As she slipped the car into gear, Lotty's words came back to her.

We're different people now.

She hoped so, because if that were true, it was the only hope she had to reach Devon, to make him change his mind.

She headed down Dune Road. His car was not in the driveway as she pulled up in front of the big Victorian. She observed the house for any signs of life before knocking. The draperies were shut, but Brooke nevertheless tried to peek through the crack to see inside. The house was dark, deserted.

She made her way around back, her heels crunching on the crushed-rock walkway. Peering through the kitchen window, what she saw made her insides churn. The countertops were completely clean, devoid of anything that would even remotely indicate that someone lived here. The refrigerator door was cracked open, the plug hanging over the top. The house looked not only empty, but abandoned.

Brooke stood stock-still. She put a hand to her chest, unconsciously attempting to calm the rising panic. She turned toward the end of the jetty. The Jet Ski was gone, the rope that secured it to the dock flapping in the early morning breeze. She watched it undulate back and forth, almost mocking her as it verified what she already knew to be true.

Devon was gone.

I could clear out of here in ten minutes, Brooke. Five, if I had to.

He could.

And he did.

Devon strutted down Main Street of Lenape Bay as if he hadn't a care in the world...which was pretty amazing considering that for all intents and purposes, he didn't have two nickels to rub together. As he passed people on the street, he mouthed a friendly good afternoon to those he knew and waved to those he didn't. All the time, he was very aware of their curious stares, expressions of disbelief, and the overall feeling that they had just entered the Twilight Zone.

He thoroughly enjoyed the confusion. It was one of the main reasons he decided to leave his rented car in the municipal lot at the far end of town and hoof it all the way to Pattersen Central Bank. What the hell, if he was going to throw his life away, he might as well have a good time doing it.

It was a cool, almost cold day, with the north wind coming in straight off the ocean. He breathed in the scent of the sea and smiled. It was good to be home. He felt great—better, in fact, than he thought he would when this crazy idea had hit him.

After leaving Lenape Bay like a thief in the night—which all things considered, was not an altogether inaccurate description of his departure—Devon had taken the first available plane to the coast. There had been no rhyme or reason to his thought processes that night. Brooke's version of the events of the past were so contrary to his own, he had no choice but to get away from everything and anything that reminded him of this place.

He'd needed time to think, so he'd gone back to California. When he'd told his mother his crazy idea, she'd actually hugged him, confessing that she had prayed for years that he'd give up his vendetta against the Pattersens and get on with his life. The fact that getting on with his life included Brooke only seemed to please her more.

Life was full of surprises. Devon smirked. He had thought he was so smart, so cool, so knowing back then when he'd asked Brooke out on a date. What better way to get back at Chaz than to sleep with his daughter? But Chaz had known what was going on all along. He had *allowed* them to get themselves in deeper and deeper because it served his own purposes.

When all was said and done, the three of them—he, Brooke and Chuck, too—had played right into the old man's hands. Chaz wanted Devon and his family out of Lenape Bay. His father's untimely death gave Chaz the perfect opportunity to do just that. As time went on, Devon's rebel attitude became Chaz's best tool. With each incident of defiance, Devon contributed to his own planned exile. It was as clear to him now as the nose on his face.

He loved Brooke. In many ways, he had never stopped loving her. She had been his focal point, his anchor, the reason he drove himself to succeed. He'd wanted to show her that he wasn't the bum everyone thought he was. He wanted to come home to Lenape Bay triumphant, a hero to the town. And he'd done just that. He had been a hero to many of these people. But not to Brooke. Not to the one person who meant the most.

She'd thrown the ball back into his court. Some difficult decisions and choices had to be made. He could continue his course of action and default on the loan, but without the satisfaction of revenge, there was little point to it. Chaz was dead, and that fact negated all the reasons for him to pursue the destruction of the Pattersens. Chuck and Brooke had been victims as much as he—maybe more.

Devon reached inside his breast pocket and pulled out an envelope. The little slip of paper inside represented all his earthy goods. He'd liquidated all his property into this cashier's check...and in a few minutes he was going to turn it over to Chuck Pattersen.

He laughed at the absurdity of it all. He would, in effect, be flat broke after he took that action. His future, and that of the town's, would be irrevocably linked with Maiden Point's success. What had started out as a scheme was now becoming a major chapter in his life.

Would Brooke be willing to share it all with him? She'd said she loved him, but that was before he'd left her—again. How many times could you do that to someone and still have them trust you? He didn't know, but he'd bet everything he had on the chance that they could make a life together here, at home in Lenape Bay.

Devon smiled at the bank guard as he swung open the door. He pretended to be unaware of the commotion his presence caused as he breezed past the various bank workers and headed straight for Chuck's office.

"Chuck in?" he asked the receptionist. When the woman returned a gaped-mouth nod, he continued, "Don't bother getting up. I'll announce myself."

Devon muffled a chuckle as he knocked and entered Chuck's inner sanctum.

"What the...? Devon!" Chuck rose to his feet.

Devon glanced around the room.

"Where is everyone?"

"Everyone?"

"The closing, Chuck." Devon glanced at his watch. "Am I early?"

"The closing?"

"Yes. Maiden Point. Remember?"

"Maiden Point?"

"Chuck, are you all right? You look a little peaked," Devon said.

"What are you doing here?"

"What do you mean? It's the twelfth, isn't it? Didn't you set the closing for today?"

"Yes...b-but you weren't...I mean...you went away."

"I had to go to California and clear up a few things."

Chuck sank into his oversize leather chair. "I think I'm having a heart attack."

Devon laughed. "It seems you didn't expect me, Chuck. Did you think I'd run out on you?"

Chuck looked up at him. "Brooke said—"

"What does she know?" Devon said. "You know how prejudiced she is about the project."

"She said you planned to default. Is that true, Devon?"

Devon pulled the check out of his breast pocket and laid it down on the desk in front of Chuck. "What do you think?"

Chuck studied the cashier's check for the longest moment. Devon watched as color slowly returned to his face. "I think this is the most beautiful thing I've ever seen," Chuck said solemnly. He looked into Devon's eyes. "You've saved my life."

"A talent for drama must run in the family," Devon said. "Where is your sister, by the way."

Chuck perked up. "At her office?"

"No, I checked there. She's not home, either."

"I don't know where she is, then. She hasn't been very well lately, Devon. She took your leaving very badly this time. Worse than the last. Lost weight. Crying a lot. Not like Brooke at all."

"She had enough energy to call off the closing, though."

"That was my doing. She didn't want to. She kept insisting you'd return in time. You should have seen the hell she gave the town council when they started to bad-mouth you at the meeting. A virtual tigress protecting her own. She's the only one who had faith. And she was right. You did come through in the end."

Devon was decidedly uncomfortable with the turn in the conversation. A hero was okay; a saint was something else. "Since you don't seem to need me right now, I'll take off and look for her."

Chuck rose and came around the desk.

"You love her, don't you?"

Devon's mouth turned up into a half smile. "Yeah."

Chuck extended his hand, and Devon took it. Their gazes locked as they shook.

"Thank you, Devon," Chuck said softly.

"I never thought I'd say this, but you're welcome, Chuck."

Chuck laughed with relief. "It's over, isn't it?"

Devon shook his head. "No. I think it's just really begun."

He took his leave and headed back down Main Street in the same direction he'd arrived. Only this time he wasn't paying attention to the odd glances that came his way. He was thinking about Brooke and where she could be.

Where would he go today if the tables had been turned? The answer hit him with the force of a fist to the solar plexus.

Where else, but to where it all began.

Brooke pushed the hair out of her face. The wind was blowing against her back, but she refused to turn into it. She swung her legs off the edge of the wooden dock and faced the choppy bay. The water was a November gray filled with the ominous promise of early winter.

It fit her mood. This was D Day for her. The day Devon either returned or vanished from her life forever. She'd fought a good fight, given it everything she had, every last breath of faith in him that she could scrape up, but when the morning sky had begun to lighten, she had finally admitted to herself that she had been wrong. He wasn't coming back. He wasn't going to do the right thing by the town, by her. He was what he was . . . a devil wrapped in a pretty package, all the more deadly because you couldn't help but love what you saw.

And she loved him. She loved him so much that the ache in her stomach had become a permanent part of her anatomy. She woke up with it, ate with it, slept with it. It never went away, just festered and grew as each day passed with no word from him.

She'd thought she was stronger. She truly thought that he could not hurt her as badly this time as he had before. But she had underestimated her feelings for him. This was worse...much worse than the last time. This time she'd planned a real future, an adult future, complete with the dream of living in the Victorian on the bay and raising a couple of children.

Brooke wrapped her arms around herself and bent forward. The pain was back, and she couldn't control it. She hadn't been eating, let alone sleeping, and she'd lost weight. She took a deep breath and let the sea air cleanse her. No more, she told herself. Today was the end. Today it was officially over. She would put the past behind her once and for all. There was plenty of work to do here, plenty of reasons to go on. The town and the people needed her, not to mention Chuck.

Today was a new beginning. She could feel it in her bones. It was fitting she make her commitment here where it all began....

Devon left the car on the road and walked across the dunes to the little cabin. He stopped as it came into view. This was the first time he'd seen it since that morning so long ago. He hadn't been able to bring himself to visit the place before. There had been the fear that its potent memories would break open long-healed scars. He hadn't been ready for that then. And now, it just didn't seem to matter anymore. Like his need for revenge, the cabin no longer held any power over him.

She was sitting on the edge of the dock, her legs swinging in the breeze. He watched her toss stones into the bay, staring at their descent as they disappeared under the choppy surf. Devon felt a feeling of peace wash over him at the sight. How many times had they sat there together doing the exact same thing? How many dreams had they shared here? How many kisses...each one a promise for the future.

"The place doesn't look the same, does it?" he said.

Brooke jumped at the sound of his voice. "Devon!"

He walked forward and stood in the middle of the dock, halfway between Brooke and the cabin. "It used to be gray and falling apart."

Brooke walked over to him. Her heart was beating fast, her breathing shallow. "When did you get back?"

"This morning," he said. "Remember how the roof leaked?"

"Devon." She reached up and turned his face to her. "I don't want to talk about the cabin."

"No?"

"No."

Devon examined her. "You look like hell."

"Thank you."

"You're welcome. Chuck said you hadn't been eating. I thought he was being dramatic."

"When did you see Chuck?"

"A little while ago."

"What for?"

"Is everyone crazy around here? Today's the closing on Maiden Point. Did you forget, too?"

"No, Devon. I didn't forget. You disappeared."

Devon wrapped his arms around her and pulled her close. "Miss me?"

She punched his chest. "Yes, I missed you, you idiot! Where have you been?"

"California. I had to take care of some business."

"Couldn't you call?"

He shook his head. "I didn't know if I could pull it off until late yesterday. There would have been no point in making promises I couldn't keep."

"What promises?" she asked warily.

"To make the closing payment."

"You did that? Does Chuck know?"

"I just left his office. Last time I looked he was salivating over my check."

Brooke threw her arms around his neck. "Oh, Devon! You did it! I knew you would. I told everyone you would come through for us." She pulled back. "Where did you get the money?"

"I didn't steal it, if that's what you're thinking. It's all mine. Everything I own, and then some. I'm broke, babe."

Brooke's face broke into a beatific smile.

"You don't have to be so happy about it."

"I am happy. Deliriously happy." She stood on her tiptoes and brushed her lips against his. "I've never been so happy in my entire life."

Devon's eyes darkened with desire. He slanted his mouth across hers and kissed her deeply. This was what he had been waiting for, dreaming about…possibly all his life. He pulled her body into his and pressed himself against her. She fit so perfectly, her softness cushioning him, welcoming him home. He wanted her. Now.

Sensing his urgency, Brooke whispered, "Let's go home."

"Uh-uh," he said. "Too late."

Devon took her hand and dragged her to the rear door of the cabin.

"Shall I? Or do you want to do it?"

"Do what?" she asked.

"Break the lock."

"Devon! We can't. Someone owns this cabin now. They've fixed it up."

"It looks pretty empty to me."

"They're summer people."

"Pigeons?"

"Yes."

"Pigeons don't count," he said, and proceeded to fiddle with the lock.

"Devon, I'm mayor. I can't go around breaking into houses."

"You make a lot of money at that job?"

"No. What has that got to do with anything?"

"I figure you're going to have to support me until Maiden Point gets off the ground."

"You what—"

The lock gave way. He grinned. "Hey, I'm getting real good at this. If the project fails, I can always become a professional—"

"Thief?"

"How little faith! I was going to say locksmith." He swung the door open. "Come here, woman."

Brooke laughed. "You're a lunatic."

"Not crazy. Free," he said as he shut the door behind them. "I've got nothing left to lose, babe." He leaned against the door. "Only you."

"That's impossible. I love you," she said, and held out her arms to him.

Devon walked toward her. He took her into his arms and kissed her, then pulled back. "Not here," he said.

He moved them toward the center of the room, to the exact spot where they had made love for the first time so many years ago. There was one more demon to exorcise. "Here."

Brooke grinned up at him. "Are you sure this is it? I think we were a little more to the left."

"No, I remember every single detail of that night. This is it."

He bent his head to kiss her, but she put a hand to his chest to stop him. "You're absolutely sure now? I wouldn't want to be a centimeter off."

"Shut up, Brooke," he said.

This time, when he kissed her, she responded with all she had to give. He tasted so wonderfully familiar, it awakened her senses to all that was to follow. Her body began to blossom as he pulled them down onto the floor.

Devon undressed her slowly, relishing the feel of his hands on her smooth skin as they glided over her naked body. "You are so beautiful," he whispered. "Tell me what you want me to do," he said.

Brooke writhed beneath his touch. "Everything," she said. "Everything and anything you want."

Devon stood and undressed. Brooke watched the autumn sun bathe his body in golden lights. He was so handsome, so magnificently masculine, that her insides churned with anticipation.

"Come to me, Devon. Love me."

He lay down next to her and buried his face in her neck. "I do love you, babe." He kissed her eyes, her cheeks, her lips. "So much..."

She parted her lips, and he wasted no time taking advantage of her invitation. His tongue swept the inside of her mouth and mated with hers. His body was on fire with want and need and the realization that this time would be like no other.

This time, they were free.

This time, there was a future.

He dipped his head to kiss the tips of her breasts, nipping, licking, stroking them to hard buds with his tongue. Brooke grabbed handfuls of his hair in her fists as she controlled the movement of his head. He traveled lower, showering her with hot, wet kisses across her belly and below, to the honey-brown nest of curls at her center.

Nestling himself between her legs, he separated her with his thumbs before touching her ever so slightly with the tip of his tongue. Brooke groaned and arched with the contact, but Devon did not relent. Instead he kissed her intimately, tasting her woman's essence, lifting her hips in his hands as he feasted on her.

Brooke bucked beneath the onslaught of his mouth, wanting him to stop...wanting him to never stop... wanting him. The explosion came suddenly, more powerful than any she had ever experienced. She cried out his name over and over as a long, drawn-out spasm took her on a ride into ecstasy.

Devon was wild. Her taste, her scent, her undulating body had made him rock-hard and out of control. Before Brooke even stopped shaking, he positioned himself over her. He drove into her wet heat in time to absorb the aftershocks of her orgasm. The feel of her was exquisite, so purely beautiful that he had to stop for a moment to savor it.

"I love you," he whispered.

Brooke looked up into those elusive blue eyes and wrapped her legs around him, holding him securely inside her with the thoroughly conscious intent of never letting him go. "Show me," she said softly.

He did. Each movement of his body, each stroke that joined then almost separated them, only to join them again more fully, was filled with a lifetime of love. Love they missed over the years. Love that had been unrequited for so long. Beautiful, poignant love that would now last forever.

Brooke raked her nails lightly over his back and smiled at the gooseflesh her touch aroused. She lifted her face to him and kissed him, a deep, fulfilling kiss that conveyed all that was present in her soul.

Devon was lost in a haze of passion so thick and intense he didn't know who or what he was. He felt himself swell inside her, harder and thicker than he'd ever thought possible. He tried to fight it, tried to make it last longer, but it was a battle that was lost from the very beginning. With a growl that started deep within, he gave up the fight, releasing himself to the profound pleasure of sharing his body—and soul—with her.

They stared into each other's eyes, silently communicating the depth of their feelings. Brooke reached up and ran her fingers through his hair. Devon reached down and rubbed his fingers across her lips.

"Say you'll marry me," he said.

"I'll marry you," she answered.

"How many kids should we have?" he asked.

"How many kids do you want?"

"Two. Three. I don't know. Maybe four."

"I'm already thirty-three. We'd better get started."

"Maybe we already have."

They stared into each other's eyes and smiled at the thought.

"I can't wait," she whispered.

"Neither can I."

Brooke's eyes clouded with tears.

"Don't…" Devon said, and kissed the corners of her eyes.

"We've wasted so much time."

He shook his head. "No, it wasn't wasted. We were learning, growing up. I've given it a lot of thought, Brooke. It would have never worked back then. If you had gone away with me, who knows what would have happened? You would have never finished school, and I might have become the bum your father said I was. We would have ended up hating each other." He shook his head again. "No. It wasn't wasted. It was the way it was meant to be. We're together now when we're old enough to appreciate what we have."

"How did you get so smart?" She grinned at him.

"From you." He stirred inside her and moved his hips. "Maybe it's rubbing off on me."

She gave him a playful punch, then lifted her lips to his. He kissed her. "There's still something we need to settle," she said.

"What's that?"

"Guess who it was standing in my window that morning after the prom?"

"Lotty."

Brooke moved back in surprise. "How did you know?"

Devon shrugged. "It didn't take a genius to figure out if it wasn't you, it had to be her. Chuck and Lotty were a hot item back then."

"Chuck and Lotty? Lord, where was I? Lotty always was so goody-two-shoes. I never even imagined—"

"You know something? For a mayor, you're pretty naive. Maybe I will go into politics. I need a job anyway."

She bit his shoulder. "Forget it. You already have a job. Town devil."

"Devil? After all I've done? I think I'm more an *angel* in disguise." He began to move inside her again. "What do you think?"

Without any coaxing at all, Brooke followed his rhythm. "Mmm," she murmured. "Maybe. Just maybe, Devon Taylor—" she lifted her lips to him "—you're a little bit of both."

* * * * *

If you've been looking for something a little bit different,
a little bit spooky, let Silhouette Books take you on
a journey to the dark side of love with

Every month, Silhouette will bring you two romantic,
spine-tingling Shadows novels, written by some of your
favorite authors, such as *New York Times* bestseller
Heather Graham Pozzessere, Anne Stuart, Helen R. Myers
and Rachel Lee—to name just a few.

In May, look for:
FLASHBACK by Terri Herrington
WAITING FOR THE WOLF MOON by Evelyn Vaughn

In June, look for:
BREAK THE NIGHT by Anne Stuart
IMMINENT THUNDER by Rachel Lee

Come into the world of Shadows and prepare
to tremble with fear—and passion....

MEN MADE IN AMERICA

Fifty red-blooded, white-hot, true-blue hunks from every
State in the Union!

Beginning in May, look for MEN MADE IN AMERICA!
Written by some of our most popular authors, these
stories feature fifty of the strongest, sexiest men, each
from a different state in the union!

Two titles available every other month at your favorite
retail outlet.

In May, look for:

FULL HOUSE by Jackie Weger (Alabama)
BORROWED DREAMS by Debbie Macomber (Alaska)

In July, look for:

CALL IT DESTINY by Jayne Ann Krentz (Arizona)
ANOTHER KIND OF LOVE by Mary Lynn Baxter
(Arkansas)

You won't be able to resist MEN MADE IN AMERICA!